The Christmas We Found Home

A Cozy, Feel-Good, and Heartwarming
Festive Romance

Ruby Hill

Table of Contents

Chapter 1:

Big-City Pressure

Snow glittered on the sidewalks, but Olivia Parker barely noticed.

She shoved her way through the subway crowd, briefcase thumping against her hip, heels clicking a rhythm that matched the restless thud in her chest. The city smelled like roasted chestnuts and exhaust, but all Olivia saw were deadlines glowing on the screen of her phone.

Five unread emails. Three missed calls. Two calendar invites flagged as urgent.

That's the life of a marketing executive.

New York sparkled around her. Store windows were alive with red velvet bows and strings of lights, while skyscrapers reflected like crystal against the night sky. Olivia moved through it all as if wrapped in glass.

Her boss's text glared up from her phone: *Call me back ASAP.*

She exhaled hard enough to fog the air. The holidays weren't holidays anymore; they were another backdrop for the grind. She'd built her career on that grind—on the sleepless nights, flawless presentations, and refusing to crack even when pressure pressed like a vice against her chest.

Brand Strategy wasn't a company where you took breaks. It was a company where you became indispensable… or you disappeared.

By the time she reached the restaurant, she was ten minutes late, hair whipped by the wind, nerves jangling. Inside, the Midtown décor was all garlands, crystal chandeliers, and soft piano renditions of carols. Clients laughed over cocktails, her boss already holding court at the table.

Olivia plastered on her best professional smile, the one that stretched her muscles and slid into her seat as if she hadn't just run three blocks in stilettos.

The dinner passed in a blur of market share statistics, champagne toasts, and carefully calibrated charm. She chimed in at just the right moments and pitched ideas polished enough to sparkle. On the outside, she was untouchable. On the inside, exhaustion curled tight as wire.

When the last handshake ended, it was nearly midnight.

Her apartment greeted her with silence. It was sleek, minimalist, and efficient, just like everything else in her life. She dropped her heels by the door and hung her coat with precision before she sank into the sofa.

Her laptop waited on the counter, a glowing reminder of unfinished work. She should open it. She should get ahead. But her gaze snagged on the one piece of warmth in the cold lines of her apartment: a framed photograph of her Aunt Margaret.

The picture was from a Christmas long ago: The Parker Inn in the background, fairy lights tangled along the roof, Margaret's auburn hair glowing under them. She was laughing, pulling Olivia—seventeen then, awkward and impatient for the future—into the frame.

Olivia swallowed. She hadn't been back to Maplewood in years. Not since college. Not since life swept her into the city's current and didn't let go.

Her phone buzzed again. Reflex had her reaching for it, expecting her boss. But the screen told another story: *Margaret's attorney.*

Olivia froze.

The photo frame tilted slightly in her hand as the truth pressed in. Margaret, her aunt, was gone, and whatever tether had once tied Olivia to that small Vermont town was fraying fast.

***

The office smelled faintly of peppermint tea and old books.

Olivia sat across from a mahogany desk, her posture sharp though her stomach roiled. Snow swept against the window behind the attorney, flakes drifting down over the Manhattan skyline. She clutched her gloves in her lap, and the leather creased from her grip.

"Your aunt left everything to you, Ms. Parker." The attorney's voice was gentle, matter-of-fact. He slid a folder across the desk. "The Parker Inn, including the surrounding land and the accounts tied to its upkeep. It's all yours."

Olivia's breath caught. She blinked down at the paperwork, her eyes snagging on her name printed over and over. *Heir. Executor. Beneficiary.* Words that didn't belong to her, not when her life was measured in quarterly goals and client accounts.

Her aunt's face flashed in her mind. She remembered warm laughter and hands always dusted in flour from holiday baking. She always wore a scarf wound loosely about her shoulders as she bustled about the inn.

The attorney folded his hands. "Margaret loved that inn. She made sure it would stay in the family."

Olivia forced herself to breathe. "And if I can't... keep it?"

"You're under no obligation to do so. The property can be sold. In fact," he said, flipping to a page in the folder, "your aunt made arrangements with a local realtor. All that's needed is your signature."

Her fingers twitched toward the pen before she could stop herself. Sell. Of course. That was the efficient thing, the practical choice. She didn't have time to run a bed-and-breakfast. She didn't even have time to run a bath most nights.

Still, the word felt heavy, foreign.

The attorney's gaze softened. "She wanted you to have the chance to decide. That was important to her."

Chance. Olivia hadn't had one of those in years.

By the time she stepped back out into the city streets, the snow had thickened, muffling the honks of taxis and the chatter of pedestrians. She stood there for a long moment, folder tucked under her arm, the cold biting her cheeks. Somewhere inside her chest, something tugged, memories of maple-scented breakfasts, evenings by the inn's fire, her aunt's voice humming carols under her breath.

She shook it off and flagged down a cab. Nostalgia didn't close deals.

***

Maxwell was waiting when she returned to the office.

He leaned against her desk like a wolf in a designer suit, arms folded, silver hair gleaming under fluorescent lights. His smile didn't reach his eyes.

"Parker," he said smoothly. "Heard about your little windfall."

Her pulse jumped. "Sir?"

He tapped the folder tucked under her arm. "The inn. Vermont. Cozy little slice of nowhere. Word travels fast, especially when assets are involved."

Olivia forced her expression to be neutral. "It's… complicated."

"No, it's simple," Maxwell said, straightening. "You go up there, sign the papers, and hand it over to the realtor. Clean exit. You're back here where you belong." He clasped her shoulder, pressure firm enough to border on threatening. "There's a promotion in play, Parker. I'm lining up candidates now. You don't want to miss your chance."

The word echoed from earlier, sharper this time.

Olivia kept her chin high. "Of course, sir."

"Good girl," Maxwell said, with the kind of approval that felt more like a leash. "Don't let sentimentality get in the way of ambition. Not when you're this close."

When he walked away, Olivia let out a breath she hadn't realized she'd been holding. Her hands trembled against the folder, the edges biting into her palms.

Sentimentality. That's what he thought Margaret was. What Maplewood was. A weakness.

And maybe he was right.

Still, as she stared out the window at the drifting snow, Olivia couldn't stop the thought whispering at the edge of her mind: *What if he wasn't?*

***

Olivia's apartment glittered like a showroom. The polished counters, chrome fixtures, and glass walls reflected the restless city. Outside, traffic hissed over the pavement, lights blinking red and green in a half-hearted imitation of Christmas cheer.

She stood in the center of her living room, suitcase yawning open at her feet.

Her wardrobe spilled a parade of tailored blazers and pencil skirts onto the sofa. She tossed them in one by one, efficient as ever, the way she packed for client trips. Practical, sharp. Nothing sentimental. She hesitated over a wool sweater tucked in the back of her closet, one her aunt had knitted years ago in soft forest green. Her fingers brushed the yarn, caught on a loose thread.

For a moment, she almost folded it into the suitcase.

Then she shoved it back into the shadows and reached for her laptop instead.

Maplewood wasn't a vacation. It also wasn't home. It was a task.

Still, the photograph of Margaret on the mantel caught her eye again, the same one she'd stared at the night before. The older woman's laughter seemed alive in the glass, her arm looped around Olivia's teenage shoulders, her smile as warm as the inn's hearth had once been.

Olivia's throat tightened. She set the frame facedown, as if hiding it could dull the pull in her chest.

She zipped the suitcase with a sharp motion and carried it to the door.

The city pulsed beyond her windows, alive with December's endless noise: honking horns, sloshing taxis, muffled carolers. It was the rhythm she knew, the one she'd fought to master. Her territory. Her battlefield.

And yet, somewhere three states away, a small town slumbered under snowdrifts, a creaky old inn waiting with lights she could almost picture through the dark.

Olivia shook the thought away. She couldn't afford to soften now. Maxwell had made that clear.

This was business. Nothing more.

She pressed a hand to the handle of her suitcase, anchoring herself in the decision. "Quick trip," she whispered into the sterile hush of her apartment. "Sign the papers. Back to my real life."

But as she turned off the lights and headed for bed, the city outside seemed less like her real life and more like a cage of glass and steel.

And for the first time in years, Olivia wasn't entirely sure which one was the illusion—the dream she'd been chasing, or the small-town warmth she'd left behind.

Chapter 2:

First Collision

The interstate stretched into white silence, flanked by forests draped in snow.

Olivia Parker tightened her grip on the steering wheel, eyes narrowed against the swirling flurries that blurred the windshield. Her rental car's wipers squeaked in protest, struggling to keep pace with the storm.

"This is ridiculous," she muttered, leaning forward as if sheer willpower could part the snow. Manhattan traffic she could handle, but this? This was nature closing its fists around her.

The GPS on the dashboard chirped cheerfully, oblivious to the weather, "*Turn left in two miles.*"

She glanced at the clock. It was past nine already, and the sky was thick with clouds that reflected the glow of her headlights back at her like a mirror. She had hoped to reach Maplewood before dark, settle into the inn, and get this over with quickly. Instead, she was crawling at thirty miles an hour, heart hammering at every curve in the road.

Her phone buzzed in the console. She reached for it instinctively, then froze at the sight of the screen—*No Service.*

"Of course."

The tires hit a patch of ice. The car fishtailed, her body jerking as she overcorrected. For one awful second, she thought she might spin off into the trees, but the car shuddered, steadied, and then coughed.

The engine sputtered. The lights on the dashboard flickered. And then—silence.

Olivia's stomach dropped. She tried the ignition once. Twice. Nothing.

The car sat there in the middle of a snowy Vermont back road, heat fading fast, flakes swirling thick around it.

Panic prickled sharp at the edges of her chest. She'd grown up in New York, yes, but Maplewood winters were something else. She remembered the way snow could pile against doors and the way nights could sink below zero until even breath froze.

Her city boots were stylish, not practical. Her coat was wool, not down. She could already feel the cold creeping in through seams.

She sat there for a long moment, staring at the steering wheel, forcing her breath to steady. *It's fine. It's fine. Someone will come by.*

But the road was silent, buried. No headlights cut through the storm. No sound but the wind.

Finally, with a groan, she shoved open the door. Snow bit at her ankles as she stepped onto the road, her heels sinking instantly. She cursed under her breath, tugging the coat tighter around herself.

The world was white and endless, trees looming like shadows. Somewhere in the distance, she thought she heard the faint ring of a bell, or maybe it was just the wind.

"Great. Just great," she muttered, breath clouding the air.

She had taken two careful steps around the hood when another sound broke through the storm, the low rumble of an engine, steady and confident.

Headlights appeared around the bend, slicing through the snow. Relief flared, quickly tempered by wariness. Out here, she had no choice but to trust whoever stopped.

The truck pulled up beside her, tires crunching through ice. It was an old pickup, its paint scuffed but sturdy, with the bed stacked with ropes and tools. The driver's window rolled down, and a gust of warm air spilled out, carrying the faint scent of pine.

A man leaned out, broad-shouldered beneath a flannel jacket, knit cap pulled low over dark hair. His jaw was dusted with stubble, his eyes sharp even in the dim light.

"You're blocking the road," he said, voice low and edged with amusement. "That's a dangerous place for a city car to quit."

Olivia bristled. "Excuse me?"

The man tilted his head toward the lifeless sedan. "Looks like she's not going anywhere."

Her teeth clenched. "She has a name. Well, technically a rental ID number, but still."

One of his brows rose. The corner of his mouth almost—*almost*—tipped toward a smile. "You from around here?"

"No," she snapped, hugging her coat tighter. "I'm heading to Maplewood. And I don't need commentary, I need a tow truck."

His gaze flicked over her with her heels sinking in the snow, her polished coat, and bare hands turning red against the cold. "Right," he said slowly. "Because there are so many of those just waiting around in the middle of a Vermont back road at night."

Olivia glared. "Do you always stop just to mock stranded women, or is tonight a special occasion?"

The man chuckled, low and warm despite the storm. "Lady, if I wanted to mock you, I'd have started with your shoes."

Her mouth fell open, a retort caught on her tongue.

And just like that, the collision began.

***

The man killed his engine, snow settling on the brim of his cap as he stepped down from the truck. Up close, he looked even more like the landscape he'd driven out of. He was broad through the shoulders, easy in the knees despite the ice, and had a kind of steady competence that made Olivia's irritation feel suddenly... juvenile.

He tipped his chin at her car. "Pop the hood."

"I'm not sure that's necessary," Olivia said, even as she fumbled for the latch and propped the hood with numb fingers. Steam breathed up into the night and vanished. The engine looked like a black, inscrutable riddle.

He leaned in, a flashlight clicking on in his hand. "Battery's freezing up. Alternator's not thrilled, either. You're lucky you didn't slide into the ditch on that bend."

"I didn't slide," she said.

His mouth quirked. "You fishtailed."

"That is a form of controlled correction."

"Sure," he said mildly. "If you're a figure skater."

She swallowed a retort and watched him work. His hands were bare, the backs browned by sun that had no business being remembered in December. A scar cut pale through one knuckle. He moved with the calm economy of someone who didn't waste energy on show. It was annoying, the way competence could read as arrogance when you were cold and stranded and wearing the wrong shoes.

"Okay," he said at last, clicking off the light. "Here are your options, city car. You can sit here and wait for a tow that won't come until morning. Or we nudge your vehicle to the shoulder, and I drive you into Maplewood. There's a mechanic who'll take a look tomorrow."

Olivia bristled at the implication that she needed rescuing. "I can call a service."

He gestured at the blank strip of her phone. "You can't call anything."

"I'll walk," she said, even as another gust cut through her coat and set her teeth chattering.

He laughed—short, disbelieving. "To town? In those heels? You'll be an icicle by the time you hit the first mailbox." His head cocked, assessing. "Where are you headed in Maplewood?"

"The inn," she said before thinking to hedge.

His gaze sharpened. "Margaret's place?"

Olivia blinked. The name hit the air like a bell. "You knew my aunt?"

"Everyone knew your aunt," he said softly, something gentler sliding through his voice. "She was… good people."

The words landed in Olivia's chest like warm stones. She shifted, uncomfortable with the way a stranger's kindness could find soft spots she'd packed away. "I'm just here to—" She caught herself, lips pressing together. *Sign the papers.* The phrase was suddenly hard to say out loud, as if the snow might report her to the pines.

He didn't push. "Name's Ethan," he said instead, offering a hand that she didn't take fast enough, so he let it fall without offense. "Ethan Cole."

"Olivia Parker."

"Figured," he said, and her brows snapped together. He lifted one shoulder. "You've got her eyes."

"That's not—" She stopped. Annoyance tangled with something like embarrassment. "Listen, Ethan, I appreciate your… civic enthusiasm, but I can handle this."

His smile went wry. "I'm not enthusiastic. I'm practical. Move the car, get you warm. That's the whole agenda."

"Do you work for the town or something?"

He nodded toward the bed of his truck, where coils of chain, a toolbox, and a battered thermos shared space with a bundle of freshly cut fir branches. The scent of pine lifted on the wind and brushed her senses. "Run a Christmas tree farm up past the ridge," he said. "Cole Pines. And

I volunteer as a handyman when things break. Which is always, because winter doesn't ask permission."

A tree farmer. Of course he was. It was like the storm had conjured him from a catalog titled *Quintessential Small-Town Man*. She could practically hear the plaid singing.

He caught the direction of her look and shook his head as if he'd seen the thought pass. "Yes, I own flannel. No, I don't chop wood shirtless for fun."

Heat flared in her cheeks before she could stop it. "Please don't make this weirder than it already is."

He grinned outright then, and it changed his face—melted the reserve, warmed the edges. It made him look younger, and something in Olivia's chest went off-balance for exactly one heartbeat before she yanked herself upright.

"Keys," he said.

"What?"

"Steering's locked. I'm going to put the truck in low, give you a gentle push so you can coast to the shoulder. You brake when I tell you." He angled a look toward the ditch. "Unless you feel like testing that figure-skating theory."

She handed over the keys, bristling at the implicit trust the gesture required. He returned to his truck, backed up with all the leisure of a man parallel parking in July, then inched forward until the heavy bumper kissed the sedan. He tapped his horn twice—*Ready?*—and she slipped behind the wheel, fingers stiff on the brake.

The push was slow, cautious. Snow hissed under tires; the car drifted in a shiver of motion and settled neatly against the plowed berm. Ethan set his brake, hopped out, and wedged a pair of blocks behind her tires like a man who had done this a hundred times.

When he opened her door, a spill of blessed warm air from the truck followed him. "Heat's dying in here. Let's move."

Olivia stepped out and immediately slid; Ethan's hand closed around her elbow, steadying without grabbing. Even if he was using gloves, she could feel the warmth in his palm and the certainty in his grip, and for a beat too long, she was aware of the heat of his body in the arctic air.

"I'm fine," she said, pulling away.

"Didn't say you weren't," he replied, unbothered.

They reached the truck, and he opened the passenger door, knocking snow from the step with a gloved knuckle. She hesitated, pride rearing for a final snarl.

He arched a brow. "It's not a limo, but it'll beat hypothermia."

Her teeth clicked. "You're very sure of yourself."

"I'm sure winter's not sentimental. Get in."

Olivia climbed up, awkward in the heels. The cab was blessedly warm, air scented with pine and coffee and something faintly like cedar smoke. A wool blanket lay folded on the bench; she ignored it, even as a tremor ran through her shoulders.

"Mechanic'll be open in the morning," he said, eyes on the road. "We'll get your battery tested, see what else is cranky."

"Thank you," she said, forcing the words out in a tone that made them sound like a legal disclaimer.

"You're welcome," he said easily. After a beat: "You really came up here alone in a storm, huh?"

"I checked the forecast," she said. "It said 'flurries.'"

"In Vermont," he said dryly, "that's meteorologist for 'might eat your car.'"

She shot him a look. "Do all the locals speak in riddles?"

"Only the ones who want outsiders to live long enough to become insiders."

Her fingers tightened in her lap. "I'm not staying."

His mouth tipped. "So you said." He nodded toward the dark ribbon of road unfurling ahead. "Town's five miles. Inn's... well, you know where it is."

She didn't answer. She was acutely aware of how small the cab was, how distinct his profile looked in the dashboard glow—the strong line of his nose, the steady set of his mouth, the occasional flick of his gaze to check the mirrors like a habit of care.

She hated that she noticed any of it.

"So," he said after a quiet minute, "Olivia Parker of Manhattan. What brings you to Margaret's place at the wrong end of a snow squall?"

She stared out at the pines. "Family business."

He nodded, as if that was the only answer he'd expected. He didn't ask more, and the restraint grated. She was used to people prying, angling, and selling. His silence felt... honest.

"You always patrol the roads looking for damsels?" she said finally, wincing at how brittle it sounded.

"Only when they park sideways," he said, and the corner of his mouth lifted again.

Prickly. That was what this was. And under it, a low hum she didn't want to name.

They crested a gentle rise, and Maplewood revealed itself in a scatter of lights along the valley. Windows were glowing golden, with smoke rising straight from a few chimneys. The faint outline of a steeple was black against the snow. Olivia felt something unspool under her ribs, a memory-thread tugged loose. She yanked it tight again.

Ethan downshifted. "We'll swing by the inn, make sure the place is warm enough to land you. After that, I'll call Tom at the garage, leave a message so you're first up."

"You don't have to do that," she said.

"I know," he replied, unruffled. "I want to."

She glanced at him, thrown by the quiet certainty. "Why?"

"Because Margaret always left cookies on the stoop for the tree lot guys when we hauled in the town spruce," he said, almost to himself. "Because she kept a thermos for the kids who didn't have gloves. Because she was the kind of person who made winter feel like it was on your side." He breathed out, the faintest fog in the warm cabin light. "Seems like the sort of legacy that deserves a soft landing."

Olivia looked away first, a knot in her throat she refused to name. "I'm not my aunt."

"Didn't say you were," he answered. "Only said you're headed to her place."

The truck carried them into town, under a banner someone had strung across Main Street—WELCOME TO MAPLEWOOD—its letters dusted white, lights blinking like steady heartbeats. Olivia exhaled, not sure whether it was relief or dread that escaped into the warm cab air.

Either way, she was here.

And the first person Maplewood had sent to meet her was a man who smelled like pine and spoke like he meant what he said.

Which, frankly, she found infuriating.

Chapter 3:

Small-Town Welcome

The truck rattled to a stop in front of the inn, its porch light glowing faintly through the falling snow. Olivia pressed her palms against her knees, eager to get out, to reclaim some measure of control after the humiliating rescue.

Ethan killed the engine and looked over, calm as ever. "You'll want to let the water run a bit before you try the taps. Pipes freeze if the heat hasn't been on steady."

Olivia shot him a glance. "Do you always offer unsolicited advice to strangers?"

"Only when they're about to make a mess of things." He nodded toward the sagging porch rail. "Watch that step, too. Been loose for years."

Her jaw tightened. "Thank you, handyman of the universe."

He didn't flinch at the sarcasm. Instead, he grabbed a tool bag from behind his seat, like a man incapable of walking past a broken hinge. When he climbed out, snow dusted his shoulders, and he moved toward the porch without waiting for her.

Olivia followed, heels slipping on the packed snow. By the time she reached the steps, Ethan had already tested the railing, muttering to himself. "Knew it. Needs new bolts."

"Are you planning to fix my entire inheritance before I even step inside?" she asked, exasperated.

He glanced back, eyes glinting. "You'd prefer it collapse under you?"

Olivia bit back the reply forming on her tongue. Every word out of his mouth felt like a tug-of-war—half helpful, half infuriating. She didn't like how easily he seemed to read her, as if her city polish were nothing but a flimsy coat of paint.

The inn smelled of cedar and dust.

Olivia set her suitcase down in the foyer and let her eyes adjust to the glow of the overhead lights Ethan had coaxed back to life. The space was just as she remembered from years ago, though smaller somehow, as if her city eyes had outgrown its proportions.

The grand staircase curved upward, its banister carved with leaves and pinecones, though the varnish had dulled with age. A garland still hung along it, limp with last year's sparkle, its ribbons faded to muted gold. The reception desk bore an old brass bell, slightly tarnished, a ledger open as though her aunt might return at any moment to jot down a guest's name.

Olivia drew a slow breath. It was charming in a way that pinched at her chest, but it was also... tired. The wallpaper was peeling in the corners, and the curtains were faded by the sun. There was also a faint whistle of a draft slipping through the windowpanes. Her aunt had loved this place fiercely, but time had not been gentle.

Olivia's throat tightened. *Margaret never threw anything away. She made even flaws part of the story.*

But stories didn't pay for repairs.

She crossed to the kitchen, flipping the light switch. Fluorescents hummed reluctantly to life, revealing a cozy but cluttered space. Copper pots dangled above the stove, mismatched mugs lined the shelves, and a plate of hardened gingerbread cookies sat abandoned under a glass dome.

Her aunt's touch was everywhere, as if she'd simply stepped out for a moment and might breeze back through the swinging door with her apron strings trailing behind her.

Olivia gripped the counter. The ache that had been humming under her ribs since yesterday rose sharp again. She shoved it down, focusing instead on logistics. Repairs, cleaning, and realtor visits. That was why she was here.

The sound of tires crunching on the snowy drive jolted her back to the present.

She straightened, brushing invisible dust from her coat, and told herself it was probably Ethan circling back with more unsolicited handyman wisdom. But when the front door creaked open, the voices that spilled in were bright, lilting, unfamiliar.

"Olivia Parker?" a woman called, her tone already warm enough to wrap around her like a quilt.

Olivia blinked, stepping back into the foyer.

Three figures appeared. The first was a silver-haired woman with sparkling eyes and a knitted hat that slouched over her ears. The second, a man in suspenders carrying a basket, cheeks red from the cold. The third was a teenage girl juggling a tray of cinnamon rolls big enough to feed an army.

Olivia froze, momentarily overwhelmed by the tide of small-town energy that had swept through the door.

"We heard you were coming," the silver-haired woman said, beaming. "And mercy, look at you—all grown up. I'm Mabel Turner, and this is my husband, Hank. And this—" she nudged the girl with her elbow "—is our granddaughter, Sophie. We thought we'd stop by with a little welcome."

The girl flushed, holding out the tray. "Grandma made me bake," she confessed. "They're not perfect."

The rolls steamed, sugar glaze dripping down the sides. Olivia's stomach growled, betraying her.

"I… thank you," she said, taking the tray. The warmth seeped into her hands, startling in its comfort.

Mabel clapped her mittened hands together. "Oh, your aunt was such a dear. She'd be over the moon to see you here, carrying on the Parker tradition."

Olivia stiffened. "I'm only here briefly."

Hank chuckled, as if she'd made a charming joke. "That's what folks always say their first night. Then the town gets under your skin. Maplewood has a way of doing that."

Olivia's mouth opened, but no rebuttal came. Mabel was already bustling toward the sitting room, talking about how the garlands needed replacing and how the festival committee would be by tomorrow to "sort details."

Festival committee?

"I—wait," Olivia said, following Mabel into the room. "The festival?"

Mabel's eyes twinkled. "The Christmas Festival, dear heart. Second weekend in December, just like always. Tree-lighting Friday, market on Saturday, caroling and cocoa Sunday. Your aunt promised the inn would host the craft fair tables and the cookie exchange. Don't worry, the committee will help. We're a well-oiled sleigh."

Olivia nearly dropped the cinnamon rolls. "Aunt Margaret... promised?"

"Back in September." Mabel's voice softened. "She felt poorly but wouldn't say it out loud. Said she wanted 'one more year just the way it ought to be.'" A beat passed, tender and honest. "She believed you'd carry it on, if the time came."

A lump rose in Olivia's throat—unwelcome, too sudden. She swallowed it with the efficiency of a woman used to swallowing feelings whole. "I'm only here to handle the estate."

"Of course," Mabel said cheerfully, as if she hadn't heard. "And while you're 'handling' it, we'll make sure you've got fresh wreaths and a working coffee urn."

Sophie reappeared with a teapot and a mismatched set of mugs—one painted with a lopsided snowman, another with a fading maple leaf. Hank wrestled a handful of kindling into the fireplace, coaxing a crackle to life.

Olivia took the mug Sophie offered, the steam damp on her face. "Thank you."

"My pleasure," Sophie said, pushing a strand of hair behind her ear. "I used to wash dishes here after school. Your aunt let me keep the tips if I played carols on her old piano." She nodded toward an upright in the corner. Its keys had yellowed, but a red scarf lay folded on the bench like a memory. "She said the inn sounded better when kids made noise."

Olivia stared at the piano a moment too long. "She had a way of making everything feel… alive."

"Because she loved this place," Hank said simply. "And the people in it."

Before Olivia could answer, the front door swung wide again. Cold air gusted in along with a flurry of new voices.

"Hello, hello!" called a man in a bright red scarf. He was lanky and effusive, glasses fogged from the temperature shift. Two women trailed behind him—one with paint on her sleeves, the other with a clipboard and a pen that looked like a magic wand.

"Brought ornaments," the painter announced, lifting a cardboard box that jingled. "I'm Lina. I run the art co-op. Your aunt kept our walls in business."

"And I'm Janine," said Clipboard, already beaming at Olivia as if they were co-conspirators. "Festival chair, which is just a fancy way of saying I won't sleep until the tree lights behave. You must be Olivia." She didn't wait for confirmation. "We're thrilled you're home."

"Home—" Olivia began.

"Parker," the man in the scarf declared, sticking out a hand. "Gideon. I teach choir at the high school and occasionally bribe the town with biscotti. Your aunt's gingerbread annihilated any chance I ever had of winning the bake-off, but I bear her no ill will."

Mabel clucked. "You say that every year, then glare at the judges like a disgruntled tenor."

"Artistic passion," Gideon said gravely, then turned to Olivia with a confiding lean. "We're all in this delightful chaos together. Margaret's booking list is in the desk, and yes, the sleigh bells sometimes tangle with the extension cords, but we survive."

Olivia blinked, overwhelmed and slightly amused despite herself. "Is there… a sign-up form for all this?"

Janine lit up. "I thought you'd never ask." The clipboard appeared as if conjured, pages flipping to a hand-lettered column titled PARKER INN—FESTIVAL STATIONS. Underneath: cider station, cookie exchange, wreath table, knit-and-chat corner.

"N-no," Olivia said, fighting a rogue smile. "I mean a sign-up form for *me*. To understand what's already been promised."

Janine's pen paused. The entire group seemed to share a look that was both fond and conspiratorial.

Mabel answered for them. "What's promised is that Maplewood will help. That's the only line you need to initial."

Lina set the ornament box on the counter and lifted the lid. Handmade glass globes shone softly—snowflakes, cardinals, tiny painted cabins. She plucked one shaped like a pinecone. "Your aunt liked this one. Said it looked like the woods exhaled."

"Lina," Gideon murmured wryly, "are we trying to make her cry on night one or saving that for the town tree?"

Olivia, who was not a crier, found her eyes suspiciously hot. She inhaled, slow and steady. "Thank you for coming by. Truly. But I don't want to give the impression that I'm—"

"Staying?" Janine supplied, not unkindly.

Olivia's grip tightened on her mug. "Yes."

"Mm," Mabel said, noncommittal, which somehow felt more persuasive than any argument could have. "Well. While you're not staying, we'll need to get the spare linens laundered and the front steps salted. Sophie, text Ethan to bring bolts for that railing in the morning before he heads to the lot."

Sophie's thumbs flew over her phone. "Already done."

Olivia startled. "You have Ethan Cole's number?"

Sophie's grin was mischievous. "Everyone has Ethan's number. He hates it."

"Try being a competent person in this town," Gideon stage-whispered to Olivia. "You get voluntold into immortality."

"Also, he's single," Lina added, a shade too casually.

"Lina," Mabel warned, though amusement tugged at her mouth.

Olivia set her mug down, perhaps too carefully. "I don't need—"

"Matchmaking?" Janine's pen hovered again, eyes bright with mischief. "Perish the thought. We're merely civic-minded."

Hank poked the fire, sparks chiming up the flue. "Besides, Margaret said she hoped you'd find what she found here."

"What was that?" Olivia asked before she could stop herself.

Hank's expression was uncomplicated and kind. "A reason to breathe easier."

The kettle hissed from the kitchen again, and Sophie trotted off for more hot water. The inn settled around them with pops from the hearth accompanying the low murmur of neighbors making themselves useful. There was a soft thump as Lina and Janine started sorting ornaments at the reception desk as if they'd always belonged there.

Olivia stared at them, these strangers rearranging her night with their hands and their kindness, and felt both invaded and steadied. New York kindness came with caveats, invoices, and exchange. This felt... different. Like being folded into a blanket she hadn't realized she needed.

She cleared her throat. "The realtor is coming tomorrow."

Mabel didn't miss a beat. "Before or after the committee walk-through?"

"The... what?"

"Festival route," Janine said, pen already moving. "We mark electrical access, traffic flow, table placement. We'll keep it light for you tonight— no ladders until breakfast." Her smile turned gentle. "We know it's a lot."

"It is," Olivia said, honesty sneaking in.

Gideon patted the desk. "Then let us be the easy part."

Silence stretched, warm and full. Outside, the snow thickened, turning the windows to milk. Inside, the inn breathed like something waking— a room that made space for more than one person's agenda.

And despite herself, Olivia felt the smallest shift under her ribs, the way a door cracks before it opens.

"Okay," she heard herself say. "Show me the list."

Janine beamed as if she'd won a small war. "Atta girl."

Mabel squeezed Olivia's arm, quick and sure. "There she is."

Olivia swallowed the protest hovering on her tongue. She wasn't surrendering. She was... gathering information. That was all.

But the way the townsfolk smiled like they'd just watched a piece of her aunt's legacy step forward made it hard to pretend they didn't see something she couldn't yet.

***

The inn smelled of cinnamon and pine now, thanks to the townsfolk's deliveries.

She wrapped her arms around herself. She'd expected paperwork, maybe dust, maybe silence. Not this tidal wave of warmth, this parade of people who spoke her aunt's name like it was a blessing and looked at her as though she were part of the inheritance too.

It unsettled her. Made her want to run.

Olivia gathered her suitcase and trudged upstairs to the room her aunt had always saved for her. The wallpaper was faded, the quilt worn, but the bedspread smelled faintly of lavender. On the nightstand sat a lamp in the shape of a snowflake, its switch slightly sticky from years of use.

She sat on the edge of the bed, fingers pressed to her temples.

This was not her world. She had built her world out of glass towers, digital campaigns, and strategy decks. It wasn't perfect, but it was hers. And though tonight had thawed something she hadn't realized was frozen, she couldn't let it matter.

She whispered it aloud, as if to nail it into the air:

"Quick trip. Sign the papers. Back to my real life."

The words hung there, soft but firm. She lay back against the quilt, staring at the ceiling, listening to the storm hush the town outside.

But somewhere beneath her mantra, the sound of laughter still lingered—Mabel's twinkle, Sophie's shy grin, Gideon's booming cheer—and Olivia realized Maplewood had already begun pressing against the walls she'd built.

She closed her eyes tighter, as if that would keep it out.

Chapter 4:

Reluctant Connection

Olivia woke to the smell of wood smoke and the ache of muscles she didn't know she had.

Morning light poured through lace curtains. The storm had passed, leaving Maplewood wrapped in fresh white stillness.

For a long minute, she lay listening to the creak of settling beams and the faint crackle of the fireplace downstairs. In the distance, the toll of church bells echoed through the valley. It was peaceful in a way that made her chest tighten. She wasn't used to mornings without alarms or the ping of overnight emails.

Then the silence broke with a loud *thunk* from below, followed by a muffled curse.

Olivia blinked. *Please tell me that's not the plumbing already.*

She threw on her robe and padded down the staircase, hair tumbling loose over her shoulders. Halfway down, she froze.

Ethan Cole stood in the foyer, hammer in one hand, toolbox at his feet, sunlight striping across his flannel shirt.

He glanced up, brow lifting. "Morning, city girl."

"What are you doing here?" she demanded, tugging her robe tighter.

He gestured at the railing he'd been tightening. "Mabel texted. Said the banister was a death trap. Figured I'd fix it before you broke your neck."

Olivia crossed her arms. "You can't just walk into someone's property."

"You can when the front door doesn't lock right," he said easily. "Also on Mabel's orders. Around here, that's basically a permit."

She opened her mouth to argue, then spotted the loose bolt he was tightening. It was the one she'd nearly caught her sleeve on last night.

He noticed her glance. "You're welcome."

Olivia huffed. "I didn't say thank you."

"Didn't have to." He drove the last bolt home and tested the railing with a firm shake. "Good as new."

He set the hammer down and looked around, eyes sweeping the foyer with the casual familiarity of someone who'd been here before. "She hasn't changed much, huh?"

Olivia followed his gaze. "It's… dated."

"It's history." He brushed sawdust from his hands. "Your aunt used to host the town decorating party here. Whole place smelled like pine and sugar."

Olivia felt that tug again—the ghost of cinnamon and laughter she half-remembered from childhood visits. She pushed it away. "Well, there won't be any decorating parties this year. Once I settle the paperwork, the realtor will—"

He cut her a look, mild but pointed. "You're really selling it?"

"Of course. I live in New York. I have a job."

Ethan nodded slowly, though the set of his jaw said he didn't approve. "Guess that makes sense. Shame, though."

"Why?"

"Because this place still matters to people." He tapped the banister lightly. "Feels wrong to see it empty."

Olivia bristled. "You make it sound like I owe the town or something."

He shrugged. "Not my business."

But his tone carried the faint edge of disappointment, and it grated. "Good," she said crisply. "Because I don't."

He met her eyes, calm, unreadable. "You keep telling yourself that."

Before she could respond, the front door creaked open again, and Sophie's voice called, "Delivery for the Parker Inn!"

Ethan turned. "Perfect timing."

Behind Sophie, two local boys hauled in a fresh-cut evergreen taller than either of them. Snowflakes clung to the branches like glitter.

Olivia blinked. "What is *that* doing here?"

"Town tree rotation," Sophie said cheerfully. "Ethan brought it from his farm. Every inn, shop, and porch gets one. Part of the festival tradition."

Ethan smiled, only slightly smug. "Consider it my goodwill gesture."

"I didn't ask for a tree."

He tilted his head. "You're welcome—again."

***

The tree was enormous. Its tip brushed the ceiling, scattering snow across the old rug like a warning of impending chaos.

Olivia stared at it as if it had personally insulted her. "That's not going to fit."

"It'll fit," Ethan said. "Just needs a little finesse."

He and the two boys turned the trunk, bumping the branches against the doorframe until one of the ornaments on the hall shelf wobbled dangerously. Olivia caught it before it fell, glaring.

"Careful! That's antique."

Ethan grinned. "So is this doorway. They'll get along."

Sophie laughed, covering her mouth. "Want us to trim it, Mr. Cole?"

"Nah," he said, planting the tree squarely in the stand. "Just a haircut on the bottom."

He crouched down, pulling a small saw from his tool bag. Olivia blinked. "You carry that around?"

"Never know when a woman's going to underestimate a pine tree."

"Or when a handyman's going to overstep."

He looked up at her, eyes bright with mischief. "I don't overstep, Ms. Parker. I just get things done while other people are still making lists."

The saw bit through the trunk with a clean rasp. Olivia crossed her arms, torn between annoyance and admiration at how easily he seemed to belong in every space he entered.

When he finished, the tree stood straight and steady, filling the room with a scent so rich it almost erased the stale air of disuse.

Ethan brushed his hands off on his jeans. "There. Maplewood's finest balsam fir. You can almost hear it sighing with relief to be indoors."

"I can hear it dripping all over my rug," Olivia muttered.

He chuckled. "You'll thank me once you see it lit."

"I doubt that."

He took a step closer, close enough that she caught the scent of pine resin and soap. "You doubt a lot of things."

Her breath caught. "I'm a realist."

"You're a skeptic."

"Same thing."

"Not here," he said softly, and for a heartbeat, neither of them looked away.

Then Sophie clapped her hands. "We'll get the decorations!"

The spell broke. The kids ran back out into the snow, and Ethan turned toward the doorway. "I'll grab the box from the truck."

Olivia followed him out, the cold air biting her cheeks. "You don't have to do this, you know. The realtor's coming in a few days. I'm not—"

"Staying," he finished. "Yeah, I've heard." He opened the truck bed, revealing boxes of tinsel, lights, and ornaments stacked with the precision of someone who took joy in order.

She frowned. "You deliver trees *and* decorate them?"

"Only for stubborn people who don't know when to accept help."

"I'm perfectly capable of hanging lights."

He handed her a box that nearly knocked her backward with its weight. "Then prove it."

Olivia scowled but carried it inside. The lid popped open to reveal ornaments shaped like stars, mittens, and small wooden hearts etched with *Maplewood Christmas Festival.*

As they unpacked, Sophie returned with cookies, Hank dropped off cocoa, and within minutes the room buzzed with quiet cheer. The locals worked around her like it was a dance they'd been practicing for years, moving with ease and laughter.

Olivia tried to blend in, but every time she reached for an ornament, Ethan's hand seemed to meet hers halfway.

"Top branch needs a steady hand," he said, nodding toward the ladder.

"I'm wearing heels."

"Then maybe let me."

"I don't need rescuing."

He gave her a patient smile. "Never said you did. But I'm taller."

She wanted to argue, but when he climbed the ladder and the lights glowed to life one by one, the argument withered on her tongue.

The room filled with the soft gleam of gold and green, the scent of cinnamon and pine. For a moment, it didn't look like an inn waiting for sale. It looked like home.

Ethan stepped down, meeting her eyes again. "Not bad for free labor, huh?"

She folded her arms, fighting a smile. "You missed a spot."

"Where?"

She gestured vaguely. "Somewhere up there."

He chuckled. "You'd make a terrible supervisor."

"I'm not hiring."

"Didn't ask you to."

The banter left the air crackling, charged with something neither wanted to name.

Sophie clapped again, breaking the tension. "Looks perfect!"

Ethan grinned. "Your aunt would've said the same."

Olivia's chest tightened. "Don't," she said quietly. "Please don't make this about her."

He studied her face for a long moment, then nodded. "Fair enough."

***

The tree stood finished in the corner. It was draped in garlands and soft white lights, topped with a star Sophie had crafted from folded paper and glitter.

Everyone else had gone home, leaving the inn hushed except for the crackle of the fire. Olivia stood a few feet back, arms crossed loosely, pretending to study the decorations instead of watching Ethan coil the spare string of lights.

He moved with the kind of quiet certainty that made her restless. Nothing about him was hurried or forced. He seemed built for steadiness, the kind of man who could weather storms and mean it.

"Looks good," he said finally, glancing over his shoulder.

She nodded, keeping her tone even. "You do this every year?"

"Since I was old enough to swing a hammer," he said. "Tree deliveries, wreath hanging, whatever the town needs." He paused, then smiled faintly. "Guess that makes me Maplewood's seasonal labor force."

She smirked. "Do you ever say no to anyone?"

"Sure. Just not often."

"That must be exhausting."

"Not really," he said, looping the cord. "Some of us like feeling useful."

Something in his voice softened the words, made them heavier than they should have been. Olivia turned toward the fire, feeling suddenly exposed under the warmth.

She needed distance. She needed clarity. She needed to stop noticing the way his voice felt like the low hum of a song she half remembered.

"Thank you," she said abruptly. "For the railing. And the tree. And the unsolicited handyman work."

Ethan's mouth curved. "You're welcome."

"I didn't mean that as approval."

"I know." He stepped closer, close enough that she caught the faint scent of pine and smoke clinging to his flannel. "But you're still saying thank you. That's progress."

Her eyes lifted to his, and for a heartbeat, the air shifted. The kind of quiet that wasn't empty... it was waiting.

Ethan cleared his throat first. "You should check the chimney flue tonight. Cold air leaks in if it's stuck."

"I'll manage."

"I'll stop by tomorrow just to make sure."

"You don't need to—"

"I'll bring coffee."

She blinked, thrown by the casual certainty. "I don't drink coffee."

He smiled, eyes glinting. "Then I'll bring cocoa."

"Ethan—"

"Relax, city girl." He stepped back, voice dipping playfully again. "Just trying to keep your pipes from freezing."

She folded her arms, trying not to smile. "I can take care of myself."

He met her gaze, the flicker of firelight catching in his eyes. "Never said you couldn't. Just think maybe you don't have to all the time."

Something in her chest tugged, sharp and confusing. "I'm not staying here," she said, firmer than she meant.

"I didn't ask you to."

"You all keep assuming—"

"I don't assume anything." His voice was steady, but his gaze held hers a beat longer than comfort allowed. "But Maplewood has a way of keeping people it wants."

Olivia turned away, pretending to adjust an ornament just to break the moment. "Well, it can stop wanting me. I've got a life to get back to."

"Sure," he said softly. "Just make sure it's the one you want."

The words hung between them, like the quiet after a snowstorm. It was still, charged, and impossible to ignore.

Ethan picked up his toolbox and headed for the door. Before he left, he glanced back at the tree, then at her. "Lock your door tonight. That latch sticks when it's cold."

And then he was gone, his boots crunching down the path toward the darkening woods.

Olivia exhaled, long and uneven, staring at the glowing tree. The inn looked alive again, golden against the fading light.

She pressed her palm to her heart, willing it to slow. "Quick trip," she whispered, as if reminding herself would make it true.

But the tree lights shimmered softly in answer, and the warmth in her chest refused to obey.

Chapter 5:

The Festival Project

The next morning, Olivia woke to knocking.

She blinked at the soft light bleeding through her curtains, wondering for a moment if she'd dreamed it. That was until another, more insistent rap echoed down the hallway.

She threw on a sweater, padded to the foyer, and cracked the door open.

Mabel Turner stood on the porch, cheeks rosy, her knitted hat dusted with snow. In her gloved hands, she held a clipboard, a roll of tape, and a smile that meant business.

"Good morning, sunshine," Mabel chirped. "We've got work to do."

Olivia rubbed her eyes. "Mabel, it's not even eight."

"Exactly. Festival planning waits for no one." Mabel brushed past her, already scanning the lobby walls. "Now, where did your aunt keep her poster board? We'll need to pin up the vendor layout."

Olivia blinked. "I'm sorry—*what?*"

"The Christmas Festival!" Mabel said, her tone bright as sleigh bells. "You didn't think we'd let it slip by, did you? The whole town's counting on you."

Olivia felt her stomach drop. "Counting on me for what, exactly?"

Mabel turned, surprise flickering. "To host, dear. Margaret promised the inn months ago. The craft tables, the cocoa bar, the cookie exchange—this is our headquarters!"

Olivia gripped the banister. "She *what?*"

"I assumed she told you." Mabel looked suddenly concerned. "Oh, honey. You didn't know?"

Olivia pressed a hand to her forehead. She'd read the will, sorted the legal documents, but there'd been nothing about... hosting an entire festival.

Mabel mistook her silence for hesitation. "It's tradition," she continued gently. "Your aunt was always the heart of it. Said the festival kept Maplewood's magic alive. Last year, when she got sick, we thought she might cancel, but she said, 'Not a chance. The inn will always be home for Christmas.'"

Olivia's chest constricted. She could almost hear her aunt saying it, voice warm and firm, eyes twinkling behind those round glasses.

Mabel reached out, touching her sleeve. "We know it's a lot to step into. But if you'd rather not—"

"No," Olivia blurted, surprising them both. "I mean... I'll help. For the festival."

Mabel's smile bloomed like sunlight through snow. "That's the spirit! I knew you had your aunt's spark."

Olivia managed a weak smile. "I'm just doing it for her."

"Of course," Mabel said, not bothering to hide the twinkle in her eye.

By the time Mabel left, Olivia had been roped into a "brief meeting" with the festival committee that afternoon. She poured herself cocoa, staring at the tree still glowing faintly in the corner, and muttered, "What did I just agree to?"

***

The meeting was held at the Maplewood Community Center, a cheerful red-brick building that looked like a gingerbread house come to life. Olivia arrived bundled in her city coat, clipboard tucked under one arm, trying to project competence even as she stepped into chaos.

Inside, the room buzzed with chatter. Tables overflowed with boxes of tinsel, spools of ribbon, and thermoses of cocoa. A large poster read *MAPLEWOOD CHRISTMAS FESTIVAL – 52ND ANNUAL!*

Janine, the ever-efficient committee chair, waved her over. "Olivia! You're just in time. We're finalizing the layout and volunteer assignments."

"About that," Olivia said carefully, "I didn't realize my aunt had signed the inn up to host. I'm not sure it's… feasible."

Janine's pen froze mid-air. "Feasible?" she repeated, as if the word had never existed before in Maplewood.

Across the table, Gideon raised a brow. "The inn's the soul of the festival. You can't have Christmas without its heart."

Lina nodded, twirling a candy cane between her fingers. "It's like trying to make cocoa without sugar."

Olivia forced a smile. "I just mean it's a lot to take on. I'm not even sure where to start."

"That's the beauty of it," Janine said brightly, sliding a folder across the table. "We already have everything planned. You're just stepping in."

"Stepping in," Olivia echoed faintly, flipping the folder open. It was full of diagrams, lists, and sticky notes that read things like *CIDER STATION SET-UP: FRIDAY 8 AM* and *WREATH CONTEST – SIGN UP BY WEDNESDAY!*

Her head spun.

Mabel patted her hand. "Don't worry, dear. You've got help."

"Who's coordinating with me?" Olivia asked.

Janine beamed. "Ethan Cole, of course. Co-chair. He's already handling logistics and setup."

Olivia froze. "I'm sorry, *what?*"

"Ethan," Janine said again, oblivious to the warning tone in Olivia's voice. "You two will make the perfect team."

The room hummed with approval. Olivia, meanwhile, felt her pulse thud somewhere between disbelief and dread.

"Oh," she said weakly. "Perfect."

***

The community center smelled like sugar cookies and sawdust.

Olivia had just finished reassuring Janine that she was *thrilled*, which was only slightly less believable than snow in July, when the door creaked open behind her.

The temperature in the room seemed to shift, or maybe it was her pulse.

"Sorry I'm late," said a voice she'd recognize anywhere. It was low, steady, and threaded with that infuriating confidence that sounded like it had never once met self-doubt.

Ethan Cole stepped inside, a dusting of snow on his shoulders, his flannel sleeves rolled to the elbows, and that easy, unbothered energy that made half the town grin and Olivia grind her teeth.

Janine brightened. "Perfect timing! We were just talking about you."

Ethan shot Olivia a knowing look. "Were we now?"

"We were," Olivia said coolly, crossing her arms. "Apparently you're my co-chair."

"Co-chair, co-conspirator—same difference," he said, pulling off his gloves. "You didn't object, did you?"

"I hadn't been informed until about thirty seconds ago."

He smiled slightly. "Then consider yourself informed."

Janine clapped her hands. "Wonderful! Now that we're all here, let's dive in. Ethan, you'll handle logistics as usual—permits, lighting, setup, deliveries. Olivia, you'll take over guest coordination, vendors, and communications."

Olivia's head snapped up. "Communications?"

Gideon chuckled. "You're the marketing hotshot from New York, aren't you? Seems like a natural fit."

Olivia resisted the urge to groan. *Of course.*

Ethan leaned against the table with his arms crossed and a smirk tugging at his mouth. "Don't worry, Parker. We'll keep the heavy lifting to me."

"That's generous," she said, matching his tone. "But I assure you, I'm fully capable of managing more than emails."

"Good to hear. I'd hate to have to teach you how to use a snow shovel."

Lina coughed discreetly, hiding a smile. Mabel sipped her cocoa like she was watching her favorite soap opera.

Janine pretended not to notice the tension, or maybe she did and enjoyed it. "Splendid! I'll let you two finalize the schedule. The festival's only a week away."

"A week?" Olivia's voice pitched up. "You mean *seven days*?"

"Technically six and a half," Gideon said helpfully.

Ethan chuckled under his breath. "You'll catch on fast."

Olivia glared. "This isn't funny."

"Didn't say it was. But you've got that 'project manager in crisis' look. Thought maybe you'd appreciate a little optimism."

"What I'd appreciate," she said tightly, "is a clear division of labor."

Ethan pushed the event schedule toward her, his handwriting neat and annoyingly competent. "Already divided. I'll handle infrastructure—lighting, booths, safety checks. You handle vendors and town communication. That includes the newspaper article."

"The what?"

"The 'Welcome Back to Maplewood' piece," he said, a ghost of amusement in his tone. "They'll want to feature you. Big headline. *Parker Legacy Continues Holiday Tradition.*"

Olivia's mouth fell open. "Absolutely not."

"Too late," Mabel said from the corner. "I already told them you'd give an interview."

Ethan's eyes gleamed with unholy delight. "Smile for the cameras, city girl."

Olivia's cheeks flushed, and she took a long, slow breath through her nose. "You're enjoying this, aren't you?"

"Maybe a little," he admitted, unrepentant. "It's been years since someone argued with me about Christmas lights. Usually, everyone just agrees and brings me cocoa."

"Well, don't get too comfortable. I don't plan on being here long enough to make that a habit."

He met her eyes, something quiet flickering there beneath the teasing. "Yeah," he said softly. "You keep saying that."

The words lingered like static between them until Janine clapped her hands again. "Excellent energy! I can already tell this partnership is going to be magic."

Olivia shot Ethan a look. "Define 'magic.'"

He grinned. "The part that drives you crazy before it works."

***

By afternoon, Olivia's desk at the inn looked like a holiday battlefield with flyers, ribbon samples, and vendor contracts spread across every available surface. The scent of pine and ink filled the air.

She sat with a pen between her teeth, typing furiously on her laptop when a knock landed on the doorframe.

Ethan leaned against it, hands tucked in his jacket pockets, a crooked grin on his face. "You look like you're plotting a corporate takeover."

She didn't look up. "I'm organizing the vendor schedule."

"Same thing, isn't it?"

Olivia sighed. "Do you ever stop talking in metaphors?"

"Do you ever stop taking yourself so seriously?"

Her fingers froze on the keyboard. "Excuse me?"

He stepped inside, glancing over the chaos on her desk. "You're running this like a Manhattan product launch. Relax. It's cocoa, crafts, and carols—not a merger."

She sat back, crossing her arms. "I don't *do* chaos."

"Then you're in the wrong town."

She met his gaze sharply, but he didn't back down. If anything, he looked amused, like he enjoyed every second of her irritation.

"Did you come here for a reason," she asked, "or just to critique my management style?"

He grinned. "Both. Also brought you these."

He set a box of string lights and a clipboard on the desk. "Inventory. Need to confirm we've got enough for the porch and the vendor booths. Janine says you have a good eye for aesthetics."

Olivia frowned. "You mean she volunteered me again."

"Welcome to Maplewood."

She groaned and stood, brushing her hair from her face. "Fine. Let's get this over with."

They stepped out onto the porch. The afternoon sun shimmered off the snow, scattering diamonds across the landscape. A breeze carried the faint scent of woodsmoke from distant chimneys.

Ethan uncoiled a string of lights, testing each bulb. "You know," he said casually, "your aunt used to start decorating the minute the first frost hit. Said you could chase away half your worries with enough twinkle lights."

Olivia softened despite herself. "That sounds like her."

"She kept a box of spares behind the counter—never trusted anyone else to hang them right."

Olivia smiled faintly. "I bet she made you help."

"Every year." He smiled at the memory. "She'd supervise with cocoa in one hand and a cookie in the other. Told me I had the patience of a saint but the balance of a newborn deer."

Olivia laughed before she could stop herself; it was a small, surprised sound that felt like something unfreezing.

Ethan looked up at her, startled for a second, then smiled in return. "There it is."

"There *what* is?"

"A sense of humor. Thought maybe New York confiscated it."

She rolled her eyes, but warmth crept into her cheeks. "You're infuriating."

"Usually," he said. "But I get results."

They worked side by side, stringing lights along the porch rail. Every so often, their hands brushed when they passed a hook or bulb. Each accidental touch lingered a little too long, like the air itself held its breath.

When the last strand flickered to life, the entire porch glowed gold against the snow.

Olivia stepped back, breath catching. "It's beautiful."

"Told you," Ethan said softly. "Results."

For a moment, neither spoke. The inn gleamed like something out of a postcard. It was warm, alive, and ready for celebration.

Then Olivia remembered herself. She crossed her arms, her armor sliding back into place. "Don't get used to me being impressed. This is temporary."

Ethan's eyes glinted. "You say that a lot."

"Because it's true."

He nodded slowly. "If you say so."

He turned toward the truck, tools slung over his shoulder. "I'll be back in the morning. We'll start on the gazebo setup."

"You don't have to—"

"Co-chair," he said simply, his voice fading with the crunch of his boots on the snow. "That's what teamwork looks like."

Olivia stood there watching him go, the lights twinkling softly around her. The snow reflected in the windows, and for the first time since she arrived, the inn didn't feel like a burden. It felt like possibility.

She exhaled, rubbing her hands together for warmth. "Quick trip," she murmured. "Sign the papers. Back to my real life."

But as the lights blinked in gentle rhythm, she couldn't help wondering if maybe this was what real life was supposed to feel like.

Chapter 6:

Clash of Worlds

The next morning dawned sharp and clear, the kind of cold that made breath bloom white and the sky glow.

Olivia arrived at the gazebo in the town square, bundled in her city coat with her tablet in hand and armed with lists, charts, and a color-coded map of the festival layout. Around her, volunteers strung garlands, hung lanterns, and hummed along to tinny Christmas music playing from someone's portable speaker.

Ethan was already there, of course—early, smiling, and completely unbothered. He wore a thick green jacket, sleeves rolled, tool belt slung low like a badge of honor.

He glanced up as she approached. "Morning, city girl. Nice clipboard."

"It's a tablet," she corrected, pulling up her spreadsheet. "And we need to stay on schedule. The booth arrangement is off by three feet, which throws off the symmetry of the main walkway."

He squinted at her screen. "You measured this?"

"Yes. Twice."

Ethan chuckled. "It's a Christmas festival, not an airport runway."

"Organization doesn't kill holiday spirit," she said, adjusting her gloves. "It makes things efficient."

He gave her a slow, amused look. "You say 'efficient' like it's a synonym for 'fun.'"

"It's a synonym for 'success.'"

He leaned on a support beam, a smile tugging at his lips. "And yet somehow, the world keeps spinning on chaos and cookie crumbs."

Olivia rolled her eyes. "Some of us prefer order to… whimsy."

"Whimsy?" he echoed, pretending to be wounded. "I'll have you know this festival's 'whimsy' brings in half the town's winter income."

She blinked, surprised. "Seriously?"

He nodded, expression softening. "Local vendors, shops, tree farms, bakers. Folks count on it. Keeps spirits up through the long months."

Her tone shifted. "I didn't realize it meant that much."

"You didn't ask."

Something in the way he said it made her chest tighten. She busied herself flipping pages on her tablet. "Then we should make sure it's flawless."

He grinned. "You're not gonna relax until you alphabetize the hot cocoa vendors, are you?"

"Not unless you'd like chaos at the beverage station."

He laughed outright, low and warm. "All right, Parker. Let's see what happens when spreadsheets meet sawdust."

They spent the next hour in a tug-of-war between method and instinct. Olivia mapped booth dimensions with precision, marking corners with red tape; Ethan eyeballed measurements and moved tables by feel. When she adjusted one display by two inches, he tilted his head, unimpressed.

"You think customers will notice that?"

"I'll notice it," she said.

He grinned. "You're exhausting."

"You're infuriating."

"And yet here we are—saving Christmas."

She shot him a glare that was half annoyance, half reluctant amusement. "If you start singing carols, I'm leaving."

"No promises."

At one point, she caught him using a hammer handle to eyeball symmetry. "You can't measure with that!" she exclaimed.

He raised an eyebrow. "Worked last year."

"That's not the same as accurate."

"Accurate's overrated," he said, tapping the nail into place. "If it looks right, it is right."

"That's… horrifying logic."

He grinned again. "You say that like you don't secretly envy it."

She opened her mouth to retort, and promptly dropped her pen into the snow. Ethan crouched first, retrieving it with gloved fingers, then handed it to her without a word. His eyes met hers briefly, and for a moment, the banter stopped.

The cold air seemed to fade.

"Thanks," she said softly.

"No problem." His voice had lost its teasing edge. Instead it was low, almost gentle.

The sound of laughter from nearby volunteers snapped the moment apart. Ethan turned back to his workbench, whistling under his breath as if nothing had happened. Olivia exhaled and stared at her tablet like it could explain why her heartbeat had suddenly gone off-script.

***

By midday, the town square had turned into organized chaos with strings of lights coiled across the snow, half-assembled booths standing like little houses waiting for roofs.

Olivia stood at the center, clipboard in hand, directing volunteers like a general preparing for battle. "Booth three goes *here*, not next to the cocoa stand or you'll block the fire pit! And please keep the decorations consistent. White lights only, no blinking multicolor strands!"

A chorus of *yes, ma'am* rose from the teens hanging garland. Ethan, meanwhile, was on the ladder across the square, casually looping lights around the gazebo roof as if gravity didn't apply to him.

"Ethan," she called, "you're missing the symmetry on the right corner!"

He looked down, brow furrowed. "The what?"

"The alignment... your top hooks are uneven!"

He blinked at her. "You brought a ruler for Christmas lights?"

She lifted her chin. "Precision matters."

He shook his head, grinning. "Not to the people drinking cocoa under them, it doesn't."

Her hands tightened around the clipboard. "We can have both precision *and* charm."

"Or," he said, adjusting another light strand, "we can have fun and call it a day."

"Fun doesn't sell tickets."

"Neither do spreadsheets," he shot back, and she could *hear* his smile from up there.

A few nearby volunteers exchanged looks, amused, whispering like kids watching parents argue at dinner.

Olivia felt her cheeks flush. "Could you please come down here for a second?"

"Sure," Ethan said easily, climbing down the ladder. He landed with a soft thud, snow scattering under his boots. "What's wrong?"

She handed him the clipboard. "This. The booth layout. If we move the cider station five feet to the left, we can reduce foot traffic bottlenecks by twenty percent."

He glanced at the map, then at the actual square. "You really can't see it, can you?"

"See *what?*"

"That this isn't a Manhattan expo hall," he said, his tone calm but firm. "This is Maplewood. Half these booths don't line up because the kids built them, the cocoa stand leaks because it's older than I am, and the point is warmth, not perfection."

"I'm not trying to erase warmth," she said tightly. "I'm trying to make sure everything runs smoothly."

"And I'm trying to make sure it feels like Christmas, not a corporate retreat."

The words landed between them, sharper than either intended. For a long moment, the only sound was the rustle of garland and the crunch of snow under boots.

Then Ethan sighed, rubbing a hand across his jaw. "Look," he said more softly, "I get it. You plan. You organize. It's how you stay in control."

Olivia's eyes flashed. "That's not a bad thing."

"Didn't say it was. But sometimes things don't need fixing. Sometimes they just need feeling."

She stared at him, jaw tight, a dozen retorts fighting to surface, and none of them winning.

He gestured toward the square. "Your aunt knew that. Half the reason people came here was because they felt *seen*. Because she let them belong."

Olivia's throat tightened. "I'm not her."

"I know," he said quietly. "But maybe you're more like her than you think."

For a moment, neither spoke. The cold stung her cheeks; the snow glowed bright around them. Something in Ethan's expression softened, and she felt her heart stumble in response.

"Ethan…" she began, unsure what she was going to say.

But Gideon's booming voice interrupted them. "Hey, lovebirds! We're out of extension cords!"

Olivia's eyes went wide. "We're not—"

Ethan grinned, clearly delighted by her sputter. "On it, Gideon." He turned back to her, smile crooked. "See? Warmth. You just gotta let it happen."

She exhaled sharply, but a reluctant smile tugged at the corner of her mouth. "You're impossible."

"Not impossible," he said, walking backward toward his truck. "Just inconveniently charming."

She rolled her eyes, but her pulse betrayed her—fluttering wildly, like one of the blinking lights she claimed to despise.

***

By the time the sun dipped behind the hills, most of the volunteers had gone home for dinner, leaving the last stretch of setup to Olivia and Ethan. The tension that had once crackled between them now hung quieter, softened by exhaustion.

Ethan was packing tools into his truck when Olivia walked up behind him, her clipboard tucked under one arm like a peace offering.

"I looked over your lighting plan," she said finally. "It's... not terrible."

He chuckled, not turning around. "High praise coming from you."

"I mean it," she said, almost smiling. "The booth spacing works better your way. The crowd flow's more natural. It just… looks right."

He glanced over his shoulder, eyes glinting. "Careful, Parker. You almost sound impressed."

"I said *almost*."

He leaned against the tailgate, arms crossed, watching her. "You know, you don't have to keep proving you can do everything yourself. People here actually like helping."

"I'm not used to that," she admitted. "In New York, if you ask for help, someone assumes you're behind on a deadline."

He nodded thoughtfully. "Yeah, well. Around here, it's the opposite. If you *don't* ask, folks think you're about to burn out."

Her mouth tilted, not quite a smile. "Too late."

Ethan laughed softly. "Then it's a good thing you're in Maplewood."

She looked away, the warmth of his voice catching her off guard. "I'm not planning to stay, Ethan."

"I know," he said, gentle but sure. "You keep reminding both of us."

The words made her chest ache in a way she didn't like. "I just don't want anyone to get the wrong idea."

He gave her a teasing look. "About what?"

"About me," she said. "I'm here to finish what my aunt started, not—"

"Fall in love with small-town charm?"

Her eyes narrowed. "Something like that."

He grinned, unbothered. "Relax, city girl. Nobody's trying to trap you. We just like you around."

The casual honesty in his tone landed harder than she expected. For a moment, she didn't know what to do with her hands or her breath or the way the fading light brushed across his jaw.

She glanced at the glowing gazebo. "The lights look beautiful."

He followed her gaze. "They do." Then, quieter, "You make it look good, too."

Her heart skipped. "Ethan—"

He cut her off with a half-smile. "Relax. That wasn't a line."

"Good," she said quickly. "Because I don't have time for—"

"Complications?"

She exhaled, frustrated and flustered all at once. "You really like finishing my sentences, don't you?"

"Only when you start them halfway."

She glared, but couldn't hide her grin this time. "You're insufferable."

"Maybe. But you're smiling."

And she was. It surprised her more than it should have.

They stood there for a long moment, the cold air nipping at their cheeks, the town glowing softly behind them. For the first time since she'd arrived, Olivia didn't feel like an outsider looking in.

She looked down, composing herself. "I should get back. I have vendor emails to answer."

He nodded, pushing off the truck. "Don't work too late. Maplewood's got a bedtime."

"I'll try to pencil that in," she said dryly.

"Do that," he said, opening the driver's door. "And Parker?"

She paused, looking back.

He smiled, that slow, steady one that did dangerous things to her heartbeat. "You did good today."

Her voice caught. "So did you."

He nodded once, then drove off down the snowy road, taillights fading like embers.

Olivia stood there under the string lights, breath curling into the night, realizing that for the first time in years, she didn't want to rush back to her real life.

But she wasn't ready to admit that—not yet.

Chapter 7:

Holiday Traditions

The smell hit her before she even opened the kitchen door: sugar, spice, and the unmistakable tang of friendly competition.

The Parker Inn's kitchen was packed. Locals bustled around counters dusted with flour, laughter echoing off copper pots. Rolling pins clattered. Someone's frosting bag exploded. Mabel shouted directions from the oven like a general leading a battalion.

"Olivia! There you are!" she called, waving a wooden spoon like a wand. "We saved you a spot by the window."

"I'm not really—" Olivia began, but before she could finish, Sophie pressed a mixing bowl into her hands.

"Too late," Sophie said cheerfully. "You're competing now. Aunt Mabel's rules."

Olivia looked down at the bowl. "This isn't even dough yet."

"Then get stirring," Ethan's voice came from behind her.

She turned. He stood there with his sleeves rolled up and an apron tied over his flannel, grin smug and sure.

"You're baking too?" she asked.

"Defending champion, three years running."

"Oh, please," Gideon called from the next table. "Only because you bribe the judges with pine wreaths."

Ethan shrugged. "Call it cross-departmental marketing."

Mabel clapped her hands. "All right, folks! One hour on the clock! And remember: Your gingerbread house must stand on its own... no glue guns this year, Gideon."

The room erupted in laughter. Olivia shook her head, but despite herself, a smile tugged at her lips.

She followed the recipe... sort of. Her dough stuck to the counter. The roof of her house cracked down the middle. And when she tried to stand the walls upright, the icing glue slid like melting snow.

Ethan leaned over her shoulder, smirking. "You're supposed to wait for the icing to set before adding the roof."

"I *know* that," she said through gritted teeth.

He handed her a spatula. "Then why are you holding it like a trowel?"

She glared. "Do you offer unsolicited advice to everyone, or just me?"

"Just you," he said easily. "You're more fun to watch."

She almost dropped the spatula. "Excuse me?"

He winked. "Relax, city girl. I meant you're... determined."

"That's not what you said."

"Nope," he said, smile widening.

By the time the timer rang, Olivia's gingerbread "inn" leaned like it had survived a minor earthquake. Gumdrop shingles slumped down the sides. Her frosting snowman had no head.

Ethan's, of course, looked like a Christmas card with neat walls, candy windows, and a perfect pine tree piped from icing.

When the judges made their rounds, Mabel paused at Olivia's creation and blinked. "It has... character," she offered diplomatically.

Olivia burst out laughing, the sound spilling out of her like it had been waiting for months. "That's generous of you."

Ethan laughed too in a full, unguarded sound that warmed the air more than the ovens did.

When they announced him as the winner (again), he tipped his imaginary hat toward her. "Good effort, Parker. Same time next year?"

She rolled her eyes. "Not a chance."

But the way she said it didn't sound convincing.

***

Two evenings later, Olivia found herself at the town gazebo again, clutching a songbook she definitely hadn't volunteered to hold.

"How did I get roped into this?" she muttered.

"Gideon," Sophie said, adjusting her scarf. "He said every committee co-chair has to join."

Olivia glared toward Gideon, who was handing out sheet music like a mischievous conductor.

"This is extortion," she said.

Ethan appeared beside her, holding a thermos of cocoa. "Relax. Nobody expects you to hit the high notes. Just sing loud enough to scare the raccoons."

"I'm serious," she said. "I haven't sung in public since middle school."

He smiled. "Then we'll start small."

He opened his own songbook and began softly humming the first verse of *Silent Night*. His voice was deep, smooth, and unexpectedly gentle. It slipped under her guard like warm light through frosted glass.

Before she knew it, she was singing too quietly at first, then louder as the crowd joined in.

By the second verse, the entire gazebo swayed in unison. Lanterns flickered, breath steamed in the air, and laughter bubbled between verses when Gideon missed a cue.

Olivia felt herself relax. The music, the snow, and the closeness wrapped around her like something she hadn't known she missed.

Ethan caught her eye mid-song and smiled. It wasn't teasing this time; it was soft, proud, and knowing.

Afterward, the group spilled toward the cider stand for warm drinks. Olivia lingered near the gazebo, watching Sophie chase snowflakes, the square glowing gold around her.

Ethan approached, brushing snow off his coat. "You survived," he said.

"Barely."

"You even smiled once or twice."

"Rumor," she said, sipping her cider.

He leaned closer, eyes dancing. "You have something in your hair."

She blinked.

He reached out before she could protest, gently brushing a white speck from her hairline. His touch was brief, but the warmth lingered.

"There," he said, stepping back.

Her breath hitched, but she covered it with a wry tone. "You're very comfortable invading personal space."

He smiled faintly. "You're very comfortable pretending you mind."

And before she could come up with a comeback, Mabel called out from across the square: "Lovebirds, save the flirting for the tree-lighting!"

Olivia groaned. "I'm never going to live that down."

Ethan's grin widened. "I hope not."

***

The night of the tree-lighting arrived wrapped in snow and anticipation.

Crowds gathered early, and the Parker Inn gleamed with fresh garlands and wreaths. Children darted between booths, clutching candy canes, while grown-ups sipped cider and swapped stories.

Olivia stood near the stage, clipboard in hand, but for once, she wasn't using it to control anything. Everything was running smoothly. The town she'd once thought quaint now felt like something alive, and she was part of it.

Ethan found her by the cider stand, wearing that same cranberry-red flannel that had somehow become her favorite color.

"Big moment," he said. "Ready to flip the switch?"

"I think so."

He smiled. "You've done good, Parker."

She looked up at the towering tree in the square, its branches heavy with snow. "*We* did good."

He tipped his head. "You sure you're from New York? That almost sounded humble."

She elbowed him lightly. "Don't ruin it."

The mayor's voice boomed through the speakers. "And now, let's welcome the woman who helped bring this year's festival to life: Olivia Parker!"

Applause rippled through the crowd. Olivia froze, caught off guard, but Ethan nudged her gently. "Go on."

She stepped up, cheeks flushed, and found herself looking out at hundreds of faces glowing in the candlelight. "My aunt used to say this town runs on kindness," she said softly into the mic. "I think she was right. Thank you for reminding me what that looks like."

She flipped the switch.

The square exploded in gold and silver light. Gasps rose from the crowd, followed by cheers and laughter. The Christmas tree shimmered brighter than the stars above.

Ethan was the first person she saw when she turned back. He stood at the foot of the stage, smiling up at her.

When she stepped down, he met her halfway. "You belong here, you know."

She shook her head lightly. "Don't start."

"Just saying," he murmured. "Maplewood suits you."

"I'm still leaving after the holidays."

He smiled, but didn't argue. "You can tell yourself that."

They stood side by side as carolers sang beneath the lit tree, the glow painting them both in gold. Olivia's chest felt full in a way she couldn't name, like the lights had threaded something new through her, something she didn't want to let go of.

When the first snowflake drifted past her eyelashes, she whispered, "I think Aunt Margaret would've liked this."

Ethan's voice was quiet beside her. "She would've loved it. She'd be proud of you."

Olivia's eyes stung unexpectedly. She smiled through it. "You're getting good at saying things I don't want to hear."

He grinned. "And you're getting worse at pretending you don't like it."

She laughed softly, leaning just enough for their shoulders to brush.

The tree sparkled above them. The music rose. And for the first time since she'd come to Maplewood, Olivia didn't want the night to end.

Chapter 8:

Snow Day

The snow began before dawn. It was soft at first, just a glittering dust on the inn's front steps, but by mid-morning, the world had vanished behind a curtain of white.

Olivia stood at the window, cocoa cooling in her hands, watching drifts crawl higher against the porch rail. The radio crackled with a cheerful-voiced warning: *"Blizzard advisory in effect through tonight. Travel strongly discouraged."*

"Perfect," she muttered. The festival follow-up meeting had been postponed, her to-do list was melting, and the inn's generator sputtered twice before giving up.

A knock rattled the door.

Ethan Cole filled the frame, snow clinging to his jacket and hair. "Roads are closing," he said. "Power lines down on the west ridge. You shouldn't stay here alone."

"I've survived Manhattan blackouts," she said.

"Yeah? Ever chopped firewood with a flashlight?"

She hesitated. "I'll be fine."

He glanced past her shoulder at the darkened hearth. "You've got maybe two hours before the temperature drops below forty."

Her pride battled common sense for a long beat. Common sense won. Barely. "What do you suggest?"

"My place," he said simply. "It's closer to the plow routes, and the stove's still working. I can bring you back when the roads clear."

Olivia looked out at the white blur swallowing Maplewood. "This is ridiculous," she muttered, grabbing her coat.

Ethan's grin was pure triumph. "You'll thank me when you can feel your fingers again."

***

The drive was slow, headlights cutting tunnels through the snow. Ethan's truck heater groaned valiantly; Olivia sat stiffly, pretending she wasn't freezing.

"You always rescue people like this?" she asked.

"Only stubborn ones."

"Lucky me."

He chuckled. "You keep saying that like it's sarcasm."

They turned down a narrow lane lined with maples bowed under snow. The farmhouse appeared at the end, all soft yellow light and woodsmoke, like something out of a Christmas card.

When Ethan pushed open the door, warmth and the smell of cedar wrapped around her. The living room glowed with firelight and boots lined up neatly by the door. As she entered, an old dog lifted its head from a braided rug.

"You didn't mention the welcoming committee," Olivia said, smiling despite herself.

"Rusty," Ethan said, scratching the dog's ears. "He only growls at salesmen and politicians."

"Then I'm safe," she said, hanging her coat.

"We'll see."

He led her to the kitchen, which was a wide, homey space with exposed beams and a window that framed the falling snow. A kettle whistled faintly on the stove.

"Make yourself comfortable," he said. "I'll throw some wood on."

Olivia lingered by the counter, fingers trailing the worn pine surface. Everything in the farmhouse felt *lived in*, not curated, not planned, just… real.

When Ethan returned, she asked, "You built this place?"

"My dad did. I fixed it up after."

"After?"

He nodded toward the photo on the mantle. There were two smiling adults and a teenage boy, with an arm around a much younger girl.

Olivia's voice softened. "Your parents?"

"Car accident, ten years ago," he said quietly. "My sister was fourteen. Somebody had to stick around."

Her chest tightened. "That's why you stayed."

"Maplewood needed one more set of hands. She needed one more adult."

Olivia wanted to say something, but words felt clumsy against the weight of what he'd just shared. So she simply nodded, meeting his eyes. "You did good, Ethan."

He smiled, small and tired and proud all at once. "She turned out all right. Teaches art up in Burlington now."

The kettle hissed louder, cutting through the moment. Ethan moved to pour water over the cocoa powder. "So," he said lightly, "ever made dinner on a wood stove?"

"Can't say I have."

"Then you're in for an education."

She crossed her arms. "I'm warning you, I'm a terrible student."

"Yeah," he said, grin tugging at his mouth, "but I'm a patient teacher."

The storm battered the windows, wind howling through the eaves, but inside the farmhouse, it was all warmth, flickering light, and the faint, electric awareness of two people suddenly very close, with nowhere else to go.

***

By the time the stew was simmering, the windows had gone opaque with frost. The farmhouse glowed amber in the lamplight, every surface reflecting the warmth of the stove.

Olivia stirred the pot with exaggerated precision, trying to look useful. "You're enjoying this," she said.

Ethan leaned against the counter, arms folded, watching her with that half-smile that had started to feel far too familiar. "What's 'this'?"

"Trapping a helpless city woman in your survivalist den."

He snorted. "You make it sound sinister."

"It's at least mildly suspicious."

"Hey, I offered you warmth, food, and functioning plumbing."

"Ah, yes," she said dryly, "the modern trifecta of romance."

That earned her a laugh, deep and genuine. It rippled through the air, warming her faster than the fire.

Rusty thumped his tail lazily from the rug as Ethan moved closer to check the pot. His shoulder brushed hers—barely, but enough to make her pulse skip.

"Not bad," he murmured, tasting a spoonful. "Needs salt."

She reached for the shaker, but he was already there, his hand closing over hers. It wasn't deliberate; it just happened. The touch was brief, rough, and electric.

He froze. She looked up.

And just like that, the room went still.

Outside, the wind howled. Inside, the air thickened.

Ethan cleared his throat first, pulling back with a soft chuckle that didn't fool either of them. "I'll, uh… grab the bread."

Olivia exhaled, setting the spoon down before she dropped it. She busied herself with bowls, pretending her hands weren't shaking.

They ate by the fire, plates balanced on their laps. The stew was hearty and simple, the kind of food that filled more than just the stomach.

Ethan told her about growing up here, including the summer festivals, fishing trips with his dad, and the winter when his sister tried to decorate their barn with fairy lights and nearly burned down the roof. His voice softened when he talked about her.

"She was a kid," he said. "Didn't know how fragile things could be. I guess I didn't either, until I had to."

Olivia listened; her usual quips quieted. "You gave up a lot," she said finally.

He shrugged. "Maybe. But I gained something, too. Peace, I guess."

"Peace," she echoed. "That's a rare thing."

He smiled faintly. "You don't get much of that in your world, do you?"

"Not the kind that lasts."

He tilted his head. "So what keeps you running toward it?"

She hesitated, staring into the flames. "Momentum. If I stop, I might have to ask what I actually want. And that's… complicated."

He studied her for a long moment. "You ever think maybe complicated's where the good stuff is?"

She looked at him then. His eyes reflected the firelight, steady and unguarded, and for the first time, she saw the quiet strength beneath his teasing.

She smiled faintly. "You talk like someone twice your age."

He grinned. "Small towns do that to you. Too much silence. You start thinking."

"Terrifying."

"Tell me about it."

They laughed, the tension breaking just enough. The snowstorm raged outside, wind against the windows, but the world inside had shrunk to the glow of the fire and the distance between them.

After dinner, Ethan fed the flames while Olivia stacked dishes in the sink. When she returned, he'd spread a blanket on the couch and poured more cocoa.

"Sit," he said. "You've earned it."

She hesitated, then sank into the spot beside him. The couch creaked softly; the fire popped.

For a long moment, they didn't speak. Just the quiet rhythm of their breathing, the low hum of the storm.

Ethan shifted slightly, his knee brushing hers. "You know," he said quietly, "you're not what I expected."

"Oh?"

"I figured you'd melt down or boss me into alphabetizing the pantry."

She smiled. "That was plan B."

He chuckled. "You're tougher than you look."

She turned toward him. "And you're softer than you act."

His eyes flicked to hers, surprised, and something in them changed, deepened.

Neither moved.

The space between them felt alive, fragile, *waiting*.

Then a log collapsed in the fire, sending sparks spiraling up the chimney. The sound jolted them apart, and the spell broke with a nervous laugh.

Ethan ran a hand through his hair. "Guess the fire's… enthusiastic tonight."

Olivia stood quickly, tucking a strand of hair behind her ear. "I should, um… check on Rusty."

He smiled knowingly. "He's snoring."

"Then I'll… make sure he's doing it evenly."

Ethan laughed, low and warm, and she fled to the kitchen, her pulse still racing.

***

The storm deepened as night settled, wind rattling the shutters and piling drifts against the porch. Inside, the farmhouse felt suspended outside of time. There was no ticking clock and no phone buzzing, only the soft hiss of the fire.

Olivia lingered in the doorway of the living room, watching Ethan coax another log onto the embers. Rusty sighed in his sleep, the dog's paws twitching through some happy dream.

"Looks like we're here till morning," Ethan said without looking up.

"I gathered."

"You okay with that?"

She hesitated. "Ask me after the cocoa runs out."

He smiled. "Already made more."

When he handed her the mug, their fingers brushed again. This time, neither of them pulled away.

"Thank you," she said quietly.

"For what?"

"For... letting me see this." She gestured around at the fire, the farmhouse, and the evidence of a life built from persistence instead of hurry. "You make it look easy."

"It isn't," he admitted. "Some days it's lonely. Some days I wish I'd gone somewhere big and loud just to hear the noise. But then storms like this hit, and I remember why I stayed."

"Because Maplewood needed you."

"Because I needed Maplewood." He looked at her then. "And maybe because I'm too stubborn to leave what still feels right."

Something in her chest shifted again, that fragile ache she'd been pretending wasn't there. She sat beside him on the rug, the fire painting gold into her hair.

"Do you ever regret it?" she asked.

He thought for a moment. "Regret doesn't last long out here. You chop wood, fix what's broken, feed whoever shows up at your door. It keeps you honest."

"That sounds... peaceful."

"It could be." He met her gaze. "If you let it."

For a long moment, neither of them moved. The only sound was the pop of sap in the logs and the faint whistle of wind through the chimney.

Then Ethan reached forward, slowly, carefully, and tucked a strand of hair behind her ear. His fingertips grazed her cheek.

Olivia's breath caught. Her heart pounded so loud she was sure he could hear it.

He leaned closer, eyes searching hers, waiting for something—permission, maybe, or courage. The space between them thinned until she could feel the heat of his breath against her skin.

A branch outside cracked under the weight of snow. The dog barked once, sharp and sudden.

The spell broke.

Ethan pulled back, clearing his throat. "Sorry. Didn't mean to—"

"It's okay," she said quickly, too quickly. Her voice trembled just enough to betray her. "We're... tired. Long day."

He nodded, jaw tight. "You can take the bedroom. I'll stay out here."

"Ethan—"

"Storm'll pass by morning."

She wanted to tell him not to apologize, that she hadn't wanted to move either, that maybe the storm wasn't the only thing keeping her there. But the words tangled somewhere between fear and longing.

Instead, she murmured, "Good night," and slipped down the hallway.

***

In the dark, she lay awake listening to the wind ease against the walls and the faint sounds of Ethan moving in the living room. She heard the clink of the poker and the soft scrape of boots on the hearth.

When silence finally settled, she turned toward the window. The snow had stopped and moonlight spilled across the floor in silver ribbons.

Olivia whispered into the quiet, as if the house could keep her secret. "Just a snow day," she said. "That's all."

But even she didn't believe it.

Chapter 9:

Community Bonds

The snowstorm had passed, leaving Maplewood blanketed in white and sunlight so bright it made the air shimmer.

Olivia stood on Ethan's porch, coffee mug warming her hands, staring out at the world reborn. The sky stretched a sharp, impossible blue. Every branch glittered. The silence after a storm had its own sound that was soft, reverent, like the earth exhaling.

Ethan stepped out beside her, adjusting his gloves. "Roads are clear now," he said. "Town plows must've been up before dawn."

She smiled faintly. "Doesn't anyone sleep here?"

"Not when there's work to do," he said, and grinned. "C'mon. I'll drive you back before Mabel sends out a search party."

**

When they reached Maplewood, the town was already alive again. People shoveled sidewalks, children dragged sleds down Main Street, and someone had hung a sign across the gazebo: THANK YOU, VOLUNTEERS!

Olivia laughed softly. "They really don't waste time."

Ethan parked in front of the inn. "You'll get used to it."

"Don't count on that," she teased, but there wasn't much conviction behind it.

Inside, the Parker Inn smelled like cinnamon and coffee. Mabel was there, of course, already fussing over a tray of muffins.

"Look who survived the blizzard!" she cried, wrapping Olivia in a hug that smelled like flour and lavender.

Olivia laughed, letting herself sink into it. "Barely. Your handyman here dragged me out of the dark ages."

Mabel winked at Ethan. "He's good for that. And you look none the worse for wear, though I suspect a little firelight did you good."

Olivia blushed. "It was just… cozy."

"'Cozy,'" Mabel repeated, eyes twinkling. "That's how it starts."

Before Olivia could retort, Sophie bounded in, her cheeks pink from the cold. "Miss Parker! You missed the sledding tournament!"

"Sledding tournament?"

"Annual post-storm race," Sophie said proudly. "We build ramps. It's chaos."

Mabel handed Olivia a muffin. "You'll have to make it up at the Winter Market tonight. Everyone's coming."

Olivia hesitated. "Everyone?"

Mabel nodded. "That includes you, dear."

Ethan chuckled. "She doesn't take no for an answer."

Olivia sighed in mock defeat. "Fine. But I'm not racing, baking, or caroling."

Mabel smiled serenely. "We'll see."

***

Later that afternoon, Olivia helped string new lights in the inn's foyer. The rhythm of it, twisting cords, stepping back, adjusting angles, was soothing. For the first time, she realized she wasn't just passing through. She was *participating*.

When she caught her reflection in the window, she hardly recognized the woman staring back. Her hair was loose, her sweater dusted with glitter. She looked… lighter.

From the doorway, Ethan watched her quietly.

"You've got the look," he said.

"What look?"

"The Maplewood one. Like you're starting to breathe the same air as the rest of us."

She rolled her eyes. "That sounds contagious."

"Maybe it is," he said softly. "And maybe that's not a bad thing."

Something in his tone made her chest tighten, but before she could answer, Sophie called from the kitchen: "Hot chocolate's ready!"

Olivia smiled. "Saved by sugar."

***

That evening, Maplewood's Winter Market glowed like a dream. Booths lined the square, fairy lights draped from lampposts, snow crunching underfoot. The air was alive with cinnamon, roasted nuts, and the sound of children laughing.

Olivia wandered between stalls, half dazzled and half amused at how everyone seemed to know her name now. "Evening, Miss Parker," one man said as he handed her a sample of candied pecans. "Heard you helped organize the festival!"

She blinked, surprised. "Who told you that?"

He grinned. "Who didn't?"

It was dizzying—the friendliness, the warmth, the way people waved without expecting anything back. For a woman who'd built a life out of efficiency and self-reliance, this much kindness felt foreign. Dangerous, even.

She stopped at a booth selling hand-knit scarves and mittens, where an elderly woman with silver curls and sharp eyes greeted her. "You're Margaret's niece," the woman said with quiet certainty.

Olivia smiled. "Guilty."

The woman reached out, covering Olivia's hand with her own. "She was my best friend. We used to bake pies together every Thursday. She'd talk about you—how clever you were, how much you reminded her of herself."

Olivia swallowed hard. "She did?"

"Oh, yes. She was proud of you. Worried, too. Said you worked too hard for things that didn't fill you up."

The words hit like an arrow wrapped in gentleness. "She wasn't wrong."

The woman chuckled softly. "We all run from stillness, dear. But sometimes stillness is what saves us." She handed Olivia a scarf the color of a winter sky. "Here. You look like someone who forgets to stay warm."

"I can't take this—"

"It's a gift," she said, eyes kind. "From one Parker woman to another."

Olivia blinked fast, managing a trembling smile. "Thank you."

"Name's Mrs. Halpern," the woman said, patting her arm. "You stop by my porch one of these afternoons. I make the best lemon bars north of Boston."

"I might take you up on that."

"I hope you do."

As Olivia turned to leave, she spotted Ethan near the cider stand. He was laughing with a young woman who looked vaguely familiar. When he waved her over, she hesitated a heartbeat, then crossed the snowy street.

"Olivia, this is my sister, Emily," he said. "Em, meet the famous festival coordinator."

"*Famous?*" Olivia said, mock groaning. "You've been exaggerating again."

Emily grinned with the same dimples and the same teasing spark as her brother. "He's been talking about you nonstop, so you've basically become a local legend."

Ethan groaned. "Ignore her."

"I never do," Emily said, nudging him playfully. Then, to Olivia: "It's really nice to meet you. I've heard about the inn since we were kids. Aunt Margaret used to host my art club there in the summers."

Olivia brightened. "She did?"

"Yeah. She let us paint murals on her back fence. Mom nearly fainted when she saw it, but your aunt said, 'Art belongs where people can see it.'"

"That sounds like her."

"She was something else," Emily said softly. "Maplewood misses her."

For a moment, the three of them stood there in easy silence, the glow of the market painting their faces gold. Olivia felt it—the invisible thread of connection looping her into something that had started long before she'd arrived.

"So," Emily said with a mischievous grin, "when are you coming to dinner at my place? My fiancé makes lasagna that could convert saints."

Olivia laughed. "You don't have to invite me just because your brother feels sorry for the stranded outsider."

Emily shook her head. "Oh, he doesn't feel sorry for you. He's just hopelessly smitten."

"Em," Ethan warned.

Emily grinned unapologetically. "What? Everyone can see it. Even Rusty."

Olivia bit her lip, trying—and failing—not to blush. "You two really are related."

Ethan muttered, "Unfortunately."

Emily's laugh was bright and warm. "You're both welcome. Sunday night. Seven sharp."

"Deal," Olivia said, smiling despite herself.

As Emily drifted back toward the bakery stand, Olivia turned to Ethan. "She's lovely."

"She's trouble," he said, but there was affection in his voice. "Raised half by me, half by this town. I guess that makes her Maplewood's favorite."

"She seems to think the same about you."

He shrugged, embarrassed. "People here don't forget when someone shows up."

Olivia watched him for a long moment. "Maybe that's what I've been missing."

"What's that?"

"Being remembered."

Ethan's expression softened. "You're not easy to forget, Parker."

The words lingered between them, warmer than the cider, deeper than they'd admit.

The Winter Market wound down slowly, the crowd thinning as lanterns dimmed and snow began to fall again in lazy, soft flakes. Olivia helped Mabel pack up the leftover muffins, her laughter echoing off the gazebo columns.

"You sure you're not secretly from around here?" Mabel teased.

"Pretty sure," Olivia said, tying a paper bag shut. "I don't have the stamina for this level of friendliness."

Mabel chuckled. "Give it a week. Maplewood has a way of sneaking up on people."

Olivia smiled, but her chest tightened. The idea that this place might be sneaking into her heart wasn't exactly comforting; it was terrifying.

After the last booth folded up, Ethan found her by the edge of the square, brushing snow from her gloves. "Need a ride?"

"I think I can manage the three blocks."

"Come on," he said, nodding toward his truck. "You'll freeze before you get there."

She hesitated, then smiled. "Persistent, aren't you?"

"Only when it matters."

***

They drove in companionable silence, the truck heater humming softly. Maplewood glowed in the rearview mirror, a cluster of lights against the sleeping hills.

"Emily likes you," Ethan said suddenly.

Olivia smiled. "She's easy to like."

"She said you reminded her of our mom," he added after a beat.

81

"That's… sweet."

"She meant it. Strong, capable, a little too good at pretending you don't need anyone."

Olivia's breath caught. "Wow. Going straight for the therapy session, huh?"

He laughed under his breath. "She's blunt. Must run in the family."

Silence settled again, thicker this time. Olivia turned to the window, watching snowflakes blur past the glass.

"She's right, though," Ethan said quietly. "You fit here more than you think. The way you talk to people, the way the town lights up when you show up—it's not just because you're Margaret's niece."

Her throat tightened. "I think they just miss her."

"They do," he said. "But that's not what this is."

She met his eyes in the glow from the dashboard. "Then what is it?"

He smiled faintly. "You make this place feel alive again."

For a moment, neither of them looked away.

Then the truck turned into the inn's snowy drive, headlights catching the garlands swaying gently in the wind. The moment broke, but the warmth of it lingered.

Ethan parked and cleared his throat. "Market's on again next weekend. If you're still around."

Olivia unbuckled her seat belt, forcing a teasing tone. "Careful, Cole. You're starting to sound like you expect me to stick around."

"Maybe I do."

She froze, hand on the door handle.

He smiled softly. "Good night, Parker."

"Good night," she said, her voice smaller than she meant it to be.

***

Inside, the inn was quiet. The fire had burned low, the scent of cinnamon still hanging in the air. Olivia slipped out of her coat, the scarf Mrs. Halpern gave her still around her neck.

She caught sight of herself in the hallway mirror, the soft light on her face, the snow in her hair, the smile she hadn't realized was there.

"Maplewood has a way of sneaking up on people," Mabel's voice echoed in her mind.

She touched the scarf, fingers tightening around the knit.

"Just for the holidays," she whispered to her reflection.

But the words didn't sound convincing anymore.

Chapter 10:

Romantic Escalation

The Parker Inn glowed with December light. Boxes of ornaments covered the floor, strands of garland coiled like green ribbon across the banister, and the faint hum of Christmas music floated from the old radio.

Olivia stood at the center of the chaos, hands on her hips, trying to decide which part of the lobby to tackle first. "How did Aunt Margaret *do* all this every year?" she muttered.

"Easy," Ethan said from behind her. "She had me."

She turned, grinning. "Oh, so you're a professional tree decorator now?"

"Jack of all trades," he said, carrying in another box. "I'm good with lights, ladders, and keeping people from electrocuting themselves."

"That last one sounds personal."

"Let's just say Gideon once tried to plug in a twelve-foot string using a fork."

Olivia laughed. "Point taken."

They started with the new tree Ethan brought for the inn, a towering spruce that reached the ceiling beams. Olivia directed from one side, Ethan from the other, and within minutes, they were both tangled in wires.

"Hold the ladder steady," he said, climbing up.

"I am."

"Are you sure? You're wobbling."

"I'm *not* wobbling—"

The ladder shifted just enough to make her squeak. Ethan steadied it quickly, laughing. "You good?"

"Fine," she said through clenched teeth. "Perfect. Totally not about to die."

"Relax, Parker. I've got you."

Something about the words made her pulse jump.

He adjusted the star at the top, and when he climbed down, they both stepped back to look. The tree shimmered gold, ornaments catching light like captured fireflies.

"It's beautiful," she said softly.

Ethan smiled. "You did most of it."

"I did the bottom third and untangled half the lights. You did the rest."

"So we're a good team, then."

The way he said it wasn't casual. Olivia looked at him, ready with some witty retort, but the words caught when she saw the reflection of the lights in his eyes.

She looked away first. "We should do the garlands before I start sentimentalizing about pine needles."

He grinned. "Whatever you say, boss."

They worked for another hour, laughter filling the inn as they climbed, stretched, and occasionally dropped entire boxes of ornaments.

When she tried to hang mistletoe above the archway, she stretched on tiptoe but couldn't quite reach. Ethan came up behind her, his hand resting lightly on her hip as he guided the ribbon higher.

"There," he murmured.

Her breath caught. His voice was right at her ear, his warmth at her back, and for a second, neither of them moved.

Then she cleared her throat and stepped away. "Looks great."

"Perfect placement," he said, smiling faintly.

"Sure."

But when she turned, she saw his gaze linger on the mistletoe before meeting hers again, and the meaning in it made her heart stumble.

***

By late afternoon, the inn gleamed like something out of a storybook. There were garlands draped, candles glowing in every window, the smell of cinnamon and pine heavy in the air.

Olivia stood outside, admiring their work from the porch. Snow had started falling again, soft flakes twirling down like they had all the time in the world.

Ethan stepped out beside her, hands in his coat pockets. "Not bad for a city girl," he said.

She gave him a mock glare. "I'll have you know I passed Decorating 101 with honors."

"Mm-hmm. You're still holding the ribbon upside down."

She looked down and then yelped when a snowball hit her squarely on the shoulder.

He grinned. "Reflex test. You failed."

"Oh, it's *on*."

Before he could react, she scooped up a handful of snow and launched it at him. It splattered against his chest, sending a puff of white powder into the air.

"Lucky shot," he said, ducking for cover behind the porch railing.

"Strategic precision," she countered, laughing.

The world narrowed to motion and the sound of shrieks and crunching snow, along with the sting of cold on flushed cheeks. Ethan dodged left, right, returned fire, and Olivia darted behind a bench, giggling like she hadn't in years.

When one of his snowballs exploded against the side of her hat, she gasped theatrically. "You *did not* just ruin my hair!"

"You had it coming!"

"You're doomed, Cole!"

She charged forward, but he caught her mid-lunge, arms looping around her waist to keep her from tumbling into the snowbank.

For a heartbeat, everything stopped.

Her laughter faded, her hands still pressed against his chest. He was grinning, breath fogging the air between them, his fingers warm even through her coat.

"You surrender?" he asked, voice rougher than it should have been.

"Never."

She scooped up a handful of snow with one gloved hand and smeared it gently along his jaw. He froze and then laughed, tipping his head back, his breath visible in the fading light.

When he looked down again, his smile softened.

There was a smear of snow on her cheek, melting slowly, glinting in her lashes. Her laughter had quieted into something else—a tremor of surprise, maybe, or recognition.

He brushed his thumb across her cheek to wipe the snow away.

"Cold," he murmured.

Her voice came out barely above a whisper. "Not really."

The air between them shifted. No more banter, no more noise, just their breaths, mingling white against the deepening dusk.

The sound of the town in the distance seemed to fade into nothing.

Ethan's hand stayed against her cheek a fraction too long, his thumb brushing her skin in a slow, unconscious motion. She didn't step back.

He took a breath, eyes flicking to her mouth, then away again, as if afraid to ruin something fragile.

Olivia broke the silence first, her voice unsteady but playful. "I think that counts as a tie."

He smiled faintly. "If you say so."

"Let's call it mutual destruction."

"Fine by me."

The warmth in his tone undid her more than the cold ever could.

***

They trudged back to the porch, shaking snow from their coats, still laughing but quieter now—like the air had changed and neither of them wanted to admit it.

Olivia leaned against the railing, cheeks flushed pink. "You're impossible."

Ethan leaned beside her, close enough that their shoulders brushed. "And yet, here you are."

She rolled her eyes but didn't move away.

Snow drifted around them like slow confetti. The sky was deep indigo, the lights from the inn spilling soft gold over the snow.

For a long time, neither spoke. And in that silence that was comfortable, warm, and charged, something real took root.

***

The inn was quiet again by the time they came back inside. Ethan lit a few candles while Olivia set the kettle on the stove, both moving slower than usual, as if neither wanted to disturb the fragile calm that had settled between them.

The fire crackled softly in the hearth. The air smelled like cocoa and pine. Olivia stood by the counter, stirring two mugs, pretending the sound of her heartbeat wasn't louder than the wind outside.

Ethan joined her, brushing snow from his hair. "That was a dangerous game out there," he said.

"Snowball diplomacy," she replied. "We reached a truce."

He smiled. "Guess I'll have to come up with a new strategy."

"Good luck. I don't surrender easily."

"I've noticed."

He took the mug from her hand, their fingers touching briefly. The contact sent a shiver through her from something that had been quietly building since the moment she'd met him.

They carried their drinks to the sitting area. The tree lights blinked lazily, gold against green, casting soft halos across the room. Rusty snored by the fire, oblivious to the electricity in the air.

Ethan leaned back on the couch, stretching his legs toward the hearth. "You ever stop working long enough to just… exist?"

She gave a half-laugh. "Define 'exist.'"

"You know. Sitting still. Doing nothing. Letting the world move without you."

"That sounds terrifying."

"Or peaceful," he said, glancing at her.

Olivia hesitated. "I wouldn't even know where to start."

He studied her for a long moment. "You just did."

When she looked up, their eyes met. The quiet between them wasn't empty. Instead, it was full, humming. She could feel the warmth of the fire on her skin, but most of the heat was coming from somewhere else entirely.

Then, as if drawn by instinct, her gaze drifted upward.

Mistletoe. Hanging just above the archway where they sat, its green leaves swaying slightly in the draft.

Of course.

Ethan noticed her looking. His lips curved in a slow, dangerous smile. "Mabel strikes again."

"Don't you dare," she warned softly, though her voice didn't sound like a warning at all.

"Hey, I didn't put it there."

"You could still ignore it."

"Could," he said, leaning closer, "but tradition's a powerful thing."

Her pulse stumbled. "Ethan—"

He stopped just short, close enough that she could feel his breath, his voice a low rumble. "Tell me to stop, and I will."

She didn't.

For a long second, neither moved. Then his hand lifted, slowly and deliberately tracing a single line along her jaw before his lips found hers.

The kiss was soft at first, tentative, like the first fall of snow. Then deeper—steady, sure, tasting faintly of cocoa and something she couldn't name. The world outside disappeared. The wind, the fire, even her own thoughts blurred into warmth and light and the wild thrum of her heart.

When they finally broke apart, both of them were breathing too fast.

Ethan rested his forehead against hers. "That was…"

"Unexpected?" she whispered.

"More like overdue."

She laughed, breathless. "You shouldn't say things like that."

"Why not?"

"Because they make me forget this is temporary."

He searched her eyes. "Does it have to be?"

She opened her mouth to answer, but couldn't. Words failed where feeling took over.

So instead, she stepped back, forcing a smile that didn't reach her eyes. "I should get some rest."

Ethan nodded slowly, though his gaze didn't leave hers. "Good night, Parker."

She hesitated at the doorway, heart pounding, fingers brushing the mistletoe one last time. "Good night, Ethan."

When she finally disappeared down the hall, he sat back on the couch, staring into the fire. The flames flickered and hissed, throwing light across the room.

Outside, snow fell again—quiet, relentless, covering the world in something new.

Chapter 11:

Doubts and Fears

The ringtone shattered the morning quiet.

Olivia blinked awake to the glow of her phone on the nightstand, heart already skipping when she saw the name on the screen: *Caldwell & Brandt Marketing.*

Her old world, calling.

She sat up, smoothing her hair, and swiped to answer. "Hi, Maxwell."

"Olivia!" Her boss's voice came bright and brisk, the way only New York people sounded before coffee. "Where have you been hiding?"

"I've been… out of town."

"Right, right—family thing, I remember." Maxwell's tone softened, then turned sharp again. "Listen, we've been in meetings all week about the new quarter. And your name came up."

Olivia stilled. "In what context?"

"In the *promotion* context," he said. "VP of Brand Strategy. We're expanding the East Coast division. You'd be leading it."

Her breath caught. "That's… huge."

"It is. But there's a catch."

Of course there was.

"You need to be back in the city before New Year's," her boss said. "The board wants you at the January kickoff. We'll need full commitment—no remote work, no distractions."

Olivia looked out the window. Snow sparkled on the porch rail, sunlight gleaming off the inn's sign: *The Parker Inn – Est. 1958.*

"I understand," she said slowly. "And the inn—?"

"Sell it," Maxwell said, like it was obvious. "You said it's yours, right? Close it out and come home. This is the opportunity we've been grooming you for."

Home.

The word stung.

Maxwell kept talking about percentages, clients, and corner offices, but Olivia wasn't really hearing. Her eyes followed a small figure outside: Sophie, trudging through snow with Rusty at her heels, laughing at something unseen.

"I'll need a few days to think," Olivia said finally.

"Think fast," he replied. "Corporate's not famous for waiting on sentiment. Congratulations, Liv—you earned this."

When the call ended, the silence felt too big for the room.

She sat for a long time staring at her reflection in the window. The woman looking back wore a sweater that smelled faintly of cedar, hair a little wilder than it used to be, eyes softer.

VP of Brand Strategy.

It was everything she'd worked for.

So why did her chest hurt?

***

A knock startled her. Ethan's voice came muffled through the door. "You up, Parker?"

She blinked, quickly setting the phone facedown. "Yeah—one second."

He peeked in, smiling, oblivious to the storm inside her. "Sophie and I are heading to the woods to cut a few fresh pines for the festival booths. You in?"

Olivia hesitated. "I have… some things to catch up on."

His smile dimmed, just slightly. "Work stuff?"

"Something like that."

He nodded, shoving his hands in his coat pockets. "All right. We'll be back by lunch."

She managed a smile. "Be careful out there."

He gave her that warm, steady look that always made it hard to breathe. "You too, city girl."

When he left, the door clicked softly shut behind him.

Olivia pressed her palms against her knees, her mind a whirl of timelines and what-ifs.

VP of Brand Strategy. New York skyline. Deadlines. Bonuses. Prestige.

And Maplewood—firelight, laughter, one pair of brown eyes she couldn't stop thinking about.

She whispered into the quiet, "What am I doing?"

Outside, the sound of Ethan's truck faded down the snowy road, leaving only the wind and the faint echo of her own doubt.

***

By afternoon, the inn was humming again. Mabel in the kitchen, Sophie making ribbons for the festival booths, the radio crooning soft carols that filled every corner. Olivia moved through it all like a ghost.

Her mind kept looping back to that call, Maxwell's voice echoing in her head: *You've earned this. Don't let sentiment ruin your momentum.*

She was halfway through drafting an email—subject line: *Re: Promotion Discussion*—when the front door creaked open and a rush of cold air swept in.

Ethan stomped snow off his boots, a coil of pine rope slung over his shoulder. "Hey," he said easily. "We got the trees. You should've seen Sophie boss me around—girl's a general."

Olivia forced a smile. "Sounds about right."

He paused, reading something in her face. "You okay?"

"Yeah. Just catching up on a few things." She minimized the email instinctively, heart jumping.

Ethan frowned. "Work things?"

She hesitated. "Old job. They want me back sooner than expected."

He nodded slowly, jaw tightening just enough to notice. "So that's what's been eating at you."

"I wouldn't say that."

"You wouldn't have to."

The words were quiet, but they landed like a stone between them.

Olivia stood, crossing her arms. "Ethan—"

"Look, I get it," he said quickly, not meeting her eyes. "You've got a big-city life waiting for you. Fancy job, skyscraper view, people who probably don't measure success in how straight their Christmas lights are."

"That's not fair."

"Isn't it?"

Her voice sharpened. "You think I'm just going to pack up and leave because I got a phone call?"

"I think you already decided you would," he said, finally looking at her. "And maybe that's fine. Maybe this was never supposed to be more than a stopover."

The accusation stung more than she wanted it to. "I didn't plan any of this," she said quietly. "Not the inn, not Maplewood, not—" She caught herself.

"Not what?"

"Nothing."

He let out a short, humorless laugh. "Right. Nothing."

For a moment, neither spoke. Snow drifted outside the window, lazy and endless.

She hated that he looked so calm, so resigned, when she could feel the storm inside her ribs.

"It's not that simple," she said finally.

"It could be."

"How?" she asked, frustration rising. "I've worked my whole life for that job. I built everything from scratch. And you think I can just throw it all away for—"

He cut her off gently. "For what, Olivia?"

Her voice dropped to a whisper. "For something that might not last."

He studied her face, his own unreadable. "You really think that little of this place?"

"I don't—"

"Or of me?"

The silence that followed was too sharp, too heavy.

Olivia's throat ached. "That's not what I meant."

Ethan nodded once, his voice even. "You should probably finish that email."

"Ethan—"

He was already pulling on his gloves. "Festival setup starts early tomorrow. I'll take care of the booths."

"You don't have to—"

"I know." He opened the door, cold air rushing in again. "But I said I would."

The door closed softly behind him.

***

Olivia sank back into her chair, staring at the half-written email still glowing on the screen.

Her fingers hovered over the keyboard.

Dear Maxwell, I've given your offer a lot of thought—

She stopped. Deleted the sentence.

Her reflection stared back at her from the laptop screen: tired eyes, flushed cheeks, the faint outline of a garland hanging behind her.

She could still hear his voice in her head: *You really think that little of this place? Or of me?*

The cursor blinked. Waiting.

Outside, the sound of Ethan's truck faded again. This time, it didn't sound like distance. It sounded like loss.

***

The inn felt different that night.

The decorations still sparkled, the fireplace still glowed, but the warmth that had filled the place since she arrived felt thin and fragile, like it could shatter if she breathed too hard.

Olivia stood in the empty lobby long after closing, the only sound the faint tick of the grandfather clock. She'd tried to write that email again, but every time she typed a few words, her stomach twisted.

VP of Brand Strategy. New York skyline. Glass offices and catered meetings.

All the things she used to want.

She pressed her palms to the counter, eyes closing. "You should be happy," she whispered to herself. "This is what you wanted."

But her voice cracked on the word *wanted*.

Because now there was Maplewood—the hum of the café in the mornings, Mabel's laugh, Sophie's endless questions, Ethan's hands steady on a ladder, his voice saying *You belong here*.

And she didn't know how to want both.

∗∗∗

Upstairs, she wandered into her aunt's old study. It still smelled faintly of cedar and paper, a time capsule of the woman who'd made this place feel alive.

On the desk sat a box she hadn't opened before. Inside were old letters, receipts, and a faded photo of Margaret and Ethan's father standing by the inn sign the year it opened. Their smiles were broad, easy, full of something Olivia couldn't name.

Beneath it was a note in her aunt's handwriting:

To my niece, if you ever find this—You don't have to choose between doing well and doing good. Just remember which one fills you up more.

Olivia traced the words with her fingertips, tears blurring the ink.

Her aunt had known her too well.

***

Downstairs, the wind picked up, rattling the garlands on the porch. Olivia wrapped herself in a blanket and sat by the fire, staring into the flames until her eyes stung.

She replayed the fight—Ethan's quiet voice, his hurt, the way he hadn't raised it once. That was the worst part: he hadn't been angry, just disappointed.

And maybe that was harder to bear.

She pulled her knees close, the blanket slipping from her shoulders. "You're not supposed to matter this much," she whispered, though the words were meant for no one but the fire.

For a long while, she just sat there watching the flames fade, listening to the clock, feeling the quiet press in around her.

By the time she finally stood, the inn was dark except for the tree lights blinking softly in the window.

She looked at her phone one last time. The draft email still waited, blank now. The cursor blinked like a question she didn't know how to answer.

Olivia set it face down on the table.

Then she turned off the lights, whispered "Good night" to the empty room, and climbed the stairs, her heart heavier than it had been in years.

Outside, snow began to fall again.

Chapter 12:

The Holiday Market

By sunrise, the town square was already alive. Vendors in bright scarves unloaded carts of crafts and sweets, carolers tuned their voices in front of the gazebo, and the air smelled like cinnamon, pine, and snow.

Olivia stood at the center of it all, clipboard in hand, trying not to think about the tightness in her chest that had nothing to do with stress. It had been two days since she and Ethan had spoken more than polite sentences.

She'd half expected him to skip the setup. He didn't.

"Morning," he said, stepping up beside her with a coil of extension cords over one shoulder.

His tone was easy, neutral. Not cold, but not the warmth she'd gotten used to, either.

"Morning," she said.

They stood there for a beat, surrounded by the hum of laughter and bells.

He cleared his throat. "You've got the booth layout?"

"Right here." She handed him the paper. Their fingers brushed—just barely—but even that small contact was enough to make her breath stutter.

"Good. Let's get started."

And just like that, they fell into rhythm.

Ethan handled the heavy lifting—trees, wreath stands, crates of ornaments—while Olivia directed volunteers with practiced ease. They didn't need to talk much. Somehow, they always seemed to know what the other was thinking.

When the microphone failed, Ethan was already kneeling to fix the cord before she could call for him. When the garland tangled around the stage railing, she was there holding it steady without a word.

It was effortless. Natural. The way things used to feel before fear and pride got in the way.

By midday, the market was in full swing. Snowflakes drifted lazily through beams of sunlight, glinting like confetti. Children chased each other with cocoa cups; the air buzzed with music and chatter.

"Looks like a record turnout," Mabel said, bustling past with a tray of cookies.

Olivia smiled. "It's beautiful."

Mabel winked. "So are you, dear. Even if you're pretending you don't know he's been looking at you all morning."

"Mabel," Olivia hissed, flushing.

But when she risked a glance across the square, Ethan was in fact watching her from the cider stand, sleeves rolled up, hair dusted with snow. He caught her eye and, for the first time in days, smiled.

Something in her loosened.

***

Later that afternoon, they found themselves side by side again at the center of the square, finishing the final touches before the evening crowd.

Ethan adjusted a string of lights over the booth entrance while she steadied the ladder.

"Careful," she said. "Last time you nearly fell off that thing."

He smirked. "You worried about me?"

"Just protecting my festival investment."

"Sure," he said, climbing down, his grin softer now. "Whatever helps you sleep."

They both laughed, and it was real laughter this time. It felt good. Familiar.

When the lights flicked on, the square transformed: warm glow against the dusk, music swelling as people clapped and cheered. Olivia's chest filled with pride and something gentler, deeper.

She turned to find Ethan already watching her.

"Nice work, Parker."

"You too, Cole."

The easy banter was back, but underneath it was something else— gratitude, relief, longing.

For the first time since the fight, the space between them didn't feel impossible. It felt like a bridge.

But bridges, she'd learn, can break in a heartbeat.

***

The festival reached its golden hour. This was the part of the evening where the whole town shimmered under strings of light. Laughter drifted between the booths; children tugged parents toward the carousel; and the square smelled of roasted chestnuts and warm sugar.

Olivia was in her element again, efficient, focused, smiling. Every part of her training came alive in this kind of chaos.

"Booth four needs more cocoa mix," she called to Sophie. "And check the sound on the carolers' mic—it's feeding back."

Sophie saluted and ran off. Olivia turned back toward the stage, just in time to feel her phone buzz in her coat pocket.

She almost ignored it. Then she saw the name: *Maxwell Caldwell.*

Her stomach tightened.

She glanced around. Ethan was across the square helping a vendor secure a canopy. Mabel was chatting with Mrs. Halpern near the tree. The music was loud enough to give her cover.

She slipped behind one of the stalls, pressing the phone to her ear. "Boss, hi."

"Liv! I'm so glad I caught you," Maxwell's voice came, bright and brisk over the static. "Listen, great news—the buyer loved your aunt's property file. He's ready to make an offer. You just need to send over the sale confirmation by tomorrow."

Olivia's breath hitched. "Tomorrow?"

"Time-sensitive deal. Perfect timing, too. Once it's off your plate, you can head back before the New Year and step straight into your new role."

Olivia's fingers went numb around the phone. "I… haven't finalized anything yet."

"Don't overthink it," he said cheerfully. "This is a win-win. Let go of the nostalgia and come back where you belong."

Where you belong.

Olivia's throat closed around the words. She looked out from behind the booth. Ethan was there—still working, still smiling at Sophie, still steady as ever.

"This isn't nostalgia," Olivia said softly.

"What?"

"Nothing," she said quickly. "I'll review the offer tonight."

"Perfect! I'll have legal send it over." Maxwell paused. "And Liv— congratulations. This is the smart choice."

The call ended.

Olivia stood there for a long moment, phone heavy in her hand, the sound of bells and laughter blurring around her.

When she finally turned, Ethan was standing a few yards away.

He'd frozen mid-step, a coil of garland still in his hand. She knew that look. It was the quiet, searching one that always cut straight through her defenses.

"How long were you standing there?" she asked quietly.

"Long enough," he said.

Her heart sank. "It's not what it sounded like."

"Sounded like you're selling your aunt's inn," he said evenly.

"I—" She hesitated, every word suddenly fragile. "It's just an offer. I haven't decided."

He gave a short, humorless laugh. "That's the thing about offers, Parker. You don't get them unless you're looking."

"I'm not—"

He shook his head. "You don't owe me an explanation."

"Maybe not, but I want to give you one."

"Don't." His voice was gentle, but it hurt more than anger would have. "I knew this was coming. You've been halfway out the door since you got here."

"That's not fair."

"Isn't it?" He set the garland down on the bench. "You're already gone, Olivia. The rest of us are just waiting for you to admit it."

She swallowed hard. "Ethan, please—"

He stepped back. "Don't make promises you don't plan to keep."

The crowd noise rose around them while they stood frozen in the middle of it, an island of silence under the lights.

Then Ethan turned and walked away, disappearing into the glow of the market before she could say another word.

Olivia stood there long after he was gone, the phone still in her hand, the world spinning cheerfully around her.

Snow began to fall again, soft and relentless.

It felt like the whole town was celebrating something she was about to lose.

***

The square glittered like a snow globe filled with children's laughter, bells chiming, and the scent of cocoa hanging in the air. But for Olivia, everything had gone muffled. The colors, the noise, the joy… They all blurred into a kind of dream she couldn't reach anymore.

She wandered toward the edge of the crowd, numb fingers clutching her phone. Maxwell's words echoed in her head: *The smart choice.*

Ethan's voice echoed louder: *You're already gone.*

She tried to breathe through it, to focus on the festival she'd built, the one she should've been proud of. People were smiling, taking pictures under the tree she'd decorated, drinking cider under the archway she'd strung with mistletoe. It was perfect.

And she'd ruined it.

"Olivia?"

Mabel's voice pulled her back. The older woman stood near the cider stand, her brow creased with concern. "Sweetheart, are you all right? You look like you've seen a ghost."

Olivia forced a smile that felt like paper. "Just tired. Long day."

Mabel didn't buy it for a second. "Is this about Ethan?"

Olivia blinked. "How did you—"

"My dear, the man walked out of here like someone stole Christmas itself. You don't get that look from a missing extension cord."

Olivia let out a shaky laugh, then bit her lip hard to stop the tears. "It's my fault. He heard a call I didn't mean for him to."

Mabel's expression softened. "And what did he hear?"

"That I might sell the inn."

Silence. Then Mabel sighed, slow and heavy. "Well. That explains the weather in his eyes."

"I didn't mean for him to find out that way. I don't even know if I want to sell anymore."

"Then don't."

"It's not that simple," Olivia whispered. "There's a promotion waiting for me. A real one. Everything I've ever worked for. And if I stay here, I lose it all."

Mabel tilted her head. "Do you lose it… or do you trade it?"

Olivia frowned. "What's the difference?"

"The difference," Mabel said gently, "is in what you get back. Sometimes we hold onto the wrong things because they look like success. But what's the point of climbing higher if you're lonely when you get there?"

Olivia's throat ached. "I don't even know where I belong anymore."

"Maybe it's not the place," Mabel said softly. "Maybe it's the *people*."

***

Later that night, when the last booth closed and the square emptied out, Olivia walked alone beneath the lights. Snow crunched under her boots. The town she'd once seen as temporary now glowed like something alive—something that had been waiting for her to notice it.

She stopped at the edge of the gazebo, looking up at the sky. The stars were hidden behind clouds, but the world still shimmered.

From here, she could see the Parker Inn in the distance—warm, steady, familiar. Home.

The word caught her off guard.

She thought of Ethan, of how easily they'd fit together before she'd let fear speak louder than her heart.

And she thought of her aunt, of that note in the study: *You don't have to choose between doing well and doing good. Just remember which one fills you up more.*

Olivia's breath fogged the air as she whispered, "I think I finally get it."

Her phone buzzed again in her pocket. She didn't look at it this time. She let it ring, the sound small and distant against the hush of falling snow.

The lights around her flickered softly, golden and kind.

And for the first time since she arrived, Olivia didn't feel like she was running from something. She felt like she was standing still—right where she was meant to be.

Chapter 13:

Emotional Confrontation

The next morning dawned gray and brittle, the kind of winter light that made everything look sharper, colder. The holiday market still shimmered with leftover garlands and half-melted snow, but the magic of the night before had vanished.

Olivia hadn't slept. She'd watched the sunrise from her window. Her cocoa had gone cold, and her heart was heavy with everything she didn't say. Ethan hadn't come by. Not for supplies, not for setup, not for anything.

When she finally stepped outside, the air was biting. The square was nearly empty; there were just a few early risers sweeping storefronts.

She found him behind the gazebo, repairing a broken wreath stand. His truck was running, exhaust curling into the frosty air.

He looked up when she approached, but his expression didn't soften.

"Ethan—"

"Morning," he said curtly, eyes on the wreath.

"I wanted to talk."

"Don't worry about it," he said, voice steady but hollow. "You made yourself clear."

"I didn't."

"Didn't you?" He straightened, brushing snow from his gloves. "You took the call. You're selling the inn. You're leaving. What else is there to say?"

She stepped closer. "It's not that simple."

He gave a short, cold laugh. "It's always simple, Parker. You either stay or you go."

"That's not fair," she said, her voice rising despite herself. "You think walking away from my career, from everything I've built, is that easy?"

"I think it's harder to stay for something that actually matters," he shot back.

The words hit like ice.

She folded her arms, trying to steady her breath. "You don't get to tell me what matters."

"Then what does?" he demanded. "A promotion? A corner office? People who won't remember your name by next Christmas?"

She flinched. "Don't do that."

"What? Tell the truth?"

"No," she snapped. "Reduce my life to sound bites because it makes you feel righteous."

Ethan's jaw tightened. "You came here and made us believe you cared about this place, about the people, about me."

"I *do* care!"

"Then why are you leaving?"

"Because I have to!"

The silence that followed rang louder than their shouting. Snowflakes drifted between them, slow and silent, melting before they touched the ground.

Ethan looked at her like he was trying to memorize her face and forget it at the same time. "You'll always find a reason, won't you? To run when it gets real."

"That's not true."

"Then prove it."

She hesitated. The words stuck in her throat.

He nodded slowly, the disappointment in his eyes sharper than anger. "That's what I thought."

He turned away, walking toward his truck.

"Ethan, please," she said, her voice cracking.

He stopped, hand on the door handle, but didn't look back. "You don't belong here, Olivia. You'll never choose this life. And that's okay."

The way he said it broke something in her.

Then he climbed into the truck and drove off, the sound of tires on snow echoing long after he was gone.

***

Olivia stayed on that bench until her fingers went numb. The cold had seeped through her coat, but she barely noticed. All she could feel was the hollow space Ethan's words had left behind.

You don't belong here. You'll never choose this life.

He'd said it like he believed it—like she'd already proved him right.

Eventually, she stood, brushing snow from her gloves, and started back toward the inn. The walk felt longer than usual. Every corner of Maplewood looked softer now, sadder. The garlands were drooping, and the twinkle lights were dull in the daylight.

By the time she reached the porch, Mabel was waiting for her, arms crossed, face full of knowing concern. "You found him."

"I did," Olivia said. Her voice sounded scraped raw.

"And?"

"It didn't go well."

Mabel sighed. "Fights never do, dear. But sometimes they clear the snow enough to see the road again."

Olivia gave a weak laugh. "I think we might've buried it instead."

She tried to retreat inside, but Mabel's hand on her arm stopped her. "Honey, whatever you said—or didn't say—don't let fear be the loudest voice in the room."

"I'm not afraid," Olivia said, but even she didn't believe it.

Mabel gave her a long look. "Then prove *that* to yourself."

***

Upstairs, Olivia paced in her aunt's old office. The papers from Maxwell's offer sat on the desk, crisp and untouched. The words seemed to glare at her: **PROPERTY SALE AGREEMENT**.

She picked it up, reading without really seeing. *Closing by December 24.*

Christmas Eve.

The irony wasn't lost on her.

A year ago, she would've signed without hesitation. A new job, a new title, a higher floor—every rung on the ladder accounted for. But now...

Now there was Ethan. Now there was Maplewood. Now there was everything she hadn't known she needed until it was too late.

She threw the papers down and sank into the chair, head in her hands.

When the knock came, she half expected it to be Mabel again. Instead, it was Ethan.

Her breath caught.

He stood in the doorway, hat in hand, looking like a man who'd fought with himself all the way there.

"I shouldn't have said that," he said quietly.

Olivia stood. "You meant it."

"Maybe. But I didn't mean to hurt you."

She swallowed hard. "You did."

Ethan exhaled, rubbing the back of his neck. "I just—every time I start to think you might stay, something reminds me you've got one foot out the door."

"Because I do," she admitted. "I worked for years to get where I am. I can't just throw it away because you think I should."

"I'm not asking you to throw it away," he said, voice rising with emotion he could barely contain. "I'm asking you to look at what's right in front of you."

Her chest tightened. "You think I don't see it? I do, Ethan. I see *you*. I see Sophie, and Mabel, and this town that feels like a story I fell into and don't know how to end. But I also see the life I built before this. My name on something I earned. You can't just ask me to stop being who I am."

"I'm not," he said. "But you can't ask me to keep hoping for something you won't choose."

His words landed like snow—soft, but heavy.

Olivia's voice shook. "You think this is easy for me? That I don't lie awake every night wondering which choice ruins me less?"

Ethan took a step forward, then stopped. "You shouldn't have to *wonder* who you are, Olivia. That's how I know you've already decided."

Her eyes glistened. "You're wrong."

He shook his head. "Then prove it."

She opened her mouth, but no words came.

He looked at her one last time, and something in his eyes broke. "I wish things were different."

Then he turned and walked out, closing the door behind him with a final, quiet click.

Olivia stood frozen, staring at the empty doorway. The silence that followed was unbearable.

She pressed a hand to her chest, as if she could steady the ache there. "You're wrong," she whispered again. "I haven't decided."

But the papers on the desk, and the empty space where he'd stood, said otherwise.

***

The room felt colder after he left.

Olivia stood in the middle of it, staring at the door, at the way the sound of it closing had seemed to echo forever. The silence was so complete it almost hummed.

On the desk, the sale agreement waited. Beside it sat the framed photograph of her aunt, smiling in front of the Parker Inn sign. It was the same photo that had greeted Olivia on her first night here.

She crossed the room slowly, tracing her fingertips over the glass. "I'm sorry," she whispered. "I don't know how to do this."

Her reflection stared back at her: tired eyes, messy hair, the faint smudge of tears she hadn't realized were falling.

When had she become so small? So uncertain?

She sat down hard in the chair and picked up the papers. Every line felt clinical, soulless—numbers, signatures, clauses. No trace of the laughter she'd heard in these halls, the warmth that still lingered in the wood.

She read the phrase *transfer of ownership* three times before her vision blurred completely.

This wasn't just about property. It was about letting go of her aunt's legacy, of the people who'd filled the emptiness she hadn't admitted to having, of the part of herself that had begun to thaw here in Maplewood.

She pressed the heel of her palm to her eyes, shaking her head. "You wanted this, remember?" she muttered. "You wanted the promotion. The title. The life that proves you made it."

But even as she said it, her chest clenched.

Because all she could think about was Ethan's voice: *I'm asking you to look at what's right in front of you.*

And she had. And she'd pushed it away anyway.

The truth settled heavy and undeniable. She wasn't afraid of losing her career. She was afraid of what it meant to *choose happiness*—to risk it, to stay somewhere without a safety net, to love someone who made her feel seen.

And now he was gone.

***

Downstairs, the wind picked up, rattling the windows. The garland over the mantle trembled, and one of the ornaments—a little wooden heart Sophie had made—fell to the floor.

Olivia knelt to pick it up. The twine was frayed, but the carving was still there: *Home is where you're loved.*

Her breath hitched. She sat there on the rug, ornament clutched in her hand, tears finally spilling unchecked.

For the first time in years, she didn't try to hold them back.

They came hard and fast, shaking her shoulders, burning her eyes. All the things she'd buried under deadlines and promotions and perfectly managed days poured out at once.

When it was over, she stayed where she was—quiet, emptied, but somehow lighter.

Outside, the wind softened. Snow began to fall again, slow and deliberate, covering everything in a clean white hush.

Olivia set the ornament gently on the mantle, then looked toward the door.

She didn't know what she was going to do next. But for the first time, she knew what she *wanted* to do.

She just wasn't sure if it was too late.

Chapter 14:

Christmas Without Magic

The Parker Inn had never felt so still.

For days, Olivia had moved through its rooms like a ghost, careful not to linger anywhere too long. The decorations still hung, but they felt like they belonged to someone else now.

She folded the last of her sweaters into her suitcase, pausing when her fingers brushed the soft red one Ethan had teased her about. "You look like a candy cane," he'd said, laughing as she'd pretended to scowl.

Now the memory made her throat ache.

She sat on the edge of the bed, staring at the open suitcase. Outside, she could hear the faint sounds of life in town—hammers, laughter, distant carols. Maplewood was preparing for its Christmas Eve Festival.

Their festival.

Ethan had thrown himself into finishing it after their fight. She'd heard through Mabel that he was working late into the night, refusing help, sleeping barely at all. The thought made her chest tighten.

She'd wanted to go to him to apologize, to say something that would undo the last few days. But every time she tried, her pride stopped her cold.

She'd already hurt him. Showing up now felt cruel.

The inn phone rang suddenly, startling her. She reached for it before realizing it wasn't her cell, but the old rotary on the nightstand, the one her aunt had insisted on keeping.

She hesitated, then lifted the receiver.

"Parker Inn," she said softly.

"Olivia! You picked up!" Maxwell's bright New York voice filled the line. "Listen, we need those papers today if we're going to close before the holiday. I sent a courier to pick them."

Olivia's stomach turned. "Today?"

"Yup! You can leave them with the front desk or—oh! You *are* still at the property, right?"

Olivia's gaze swept the room, looking at the half-packed suitcase, the folded sweater, and the view of the snowy square through the window. "Yeah," she said after a pause. "For now."

"Good. Then let's make this official, Liv. New Year's in Manhattan, champagne in hand, VP title waiting on your desk. It's everything you've worked for."

Olivia swallowed hard. "Right."

"Congratulations, sweetheart," Maxwell added. "You're almost home."

Home.

When she hung up, Olivia stayed seated on the bed, staring at the quiet phone like it had just said something obscene.

Her reflection in the window looked pale, hollow.

Almost home.

She whispered the words under her breath. "Then why doesn't it feel like it?"

***

She carried her suitcase downstairs an hour later, leaving it by the door. Mabel was in the kitchen, baking pies for the festival dinner.

"Heading out soon?" the older woman asked gently.

"Maybe tomorrow," Olivia said, not meeting her eyes. "Once the courier picks up the papers."

Mabel nodded slowly, wiping her hands on her apron. "You'll be missed."

Olivia forced a smile. "You'll barely notice I'm gone."

"Sweetheart," Mabel said, voice soft but steady, "the whole town's noticed since you stopped smiling."

That almost broke her.

But she just nodded, mumbled something about errands, and stepped out into the cold.

The streets were full of lights, music, and laughter. Every window glowed with warmth. The air smelled of cinnamon and pine.

And yet, somehow, Christmas had never felt so far away.

***

Ethan Cole had always believed in fixing things. Broken fences, leaky pipes, cracked porch steps—there was nothing a steady hand and patience couldn't put right.

But heartbreak? That was different.

The morning after their argument, he'd thrown himself into work like it could silence the ache in his chest. The festival grounds needed final touches anyway, so he got to work on the nativity booth, the stage wiring, and the snowplow route through Main Street. There was always something to do.

So he did everything.

By the time the sun rose over Maplewood Square, Ethan had already hauled crates of decorations, repaired the hot chocolate machine, and helped Sophie hang the new star atop the Christmas tree.

"Too much?" she asked, laughing as he climbed down from the ladder.

"Never enough," he muttered, wiping his hands on his gloves.

Sophie gave him a look only little sisters could manage. It was the kind that saw through everything. "You've been at this since dawn."

"Festival's tomorrow," he said.

"Yeah, but you're not the only one planning it. You could, you know, let someone else breathe near the wreaths."

He tried for a grin. "I'm fine."

"Uh-huh," Sophie said, unimpressed. "Fine means 'I'm falling apart but I don't want to talk about it.'"

Ethan's jaw tightened. "I'm not—"

She crossed her arms. "You are."

He sighed, picking up a coil of string lights. "Drop it, Soph."

She hesitated, then softened. "She's leaving, isn't she?"

His hands stilled. "Who told you that?"

"Mabel. Said she's packing up."

Ethan looked down at the tangle of lights, blinking against the sharp sting in his chest. "Good for her," he said finally. "She deserves the city, the job, the... everything."

Sophie frowned. "You don't mean that."

"I do."

He bent to untangle the wire, but his hands shook slightly.

Truth was, he couldn't stop picturing Olivia standing at the market that night, snow in her hair, phone pressed to her ear, the look on her face when she saw him watching.

He'd tried to forget it. Tried to convince himself she wasn't different, that she was just passing through like everyone else who looked at Maplewood and saw a stopover instead of a home.

But then he'd remember her laughter—quiet and warm—or the way she'd run her hands over the worn banister of the inn like she could feel its heartbeat.

And it hurt all over again.

***

By afternoon, the festival grounds were done. The booths stood ready, the lights strung, the tree a perfect blaze of gold and red.

Ethan stood in the center of it all, exhaustion buzzing under his skin. The work should've felt satisfying. But instead, it just felt… empty.

He spotted Mabel across the square, handing out cider. She waved him over; her usual cheer had dimmed. "You've outdone yourself, Ethan."

"Just doing my part."

"You've been doing everyone's part," she said gently. "Since when does fixing everything make the heartache go away?"

He managed a faint smile. "You've been talking to Sophie."

"She's worried about you. So am I."

"Don't be," he said. "It's not the first time someone decided Maplewood was too small for them."

"But it's the first time it mattered this much," Mabel said.

He didn't respond. Just looked around the square at the lights flickering on as the sky darkened, and listened to the laughter echoing through the air.

Mabel laid a hand on his arm. "You can't keep punishing yourself for caring, Ethan. That's what makes you who you are."

He nodded, throat tight. "Doesn't make it hurt less."

"No," she said softly. "But it means your heart's still working."

She left him then, heading toward the bakery booth. Ethan stayed, watching the snow begin to fall again—quiet, steady, patient.

He closed his eyes for a moment, breathing in the cold air. It burned, but it also cleared the fog in his mind.

He didn't know if Olivia would stay. He didn't even know if she cared anymore.

But somehow, even now, he couldn't bring himself to stop caring.

***

Snow fell harder that evening, covering Maplewood in a soft white hush. The streets glowed gold under the lamplight, music drifting faintly from the square where last-minute preparations continued for tomorrow's festival.

Olivia watched from her window at the inn, her packed suitcase waiting by the door. The courier hadn't come yet. Each passing minute should have brought relief, but instead, it twisted something deeper inside her.

She traced a circle on the frosted glass. Beyond it, she could see faint silhouettes of families laughing as they carried wreaths and couples arm in arm, with lights blinking warm and steady around them.

Christmas Eve in Maplewood.

It was everything she'd helped build... and somehow, she'd never felt more outside of it.

Her phone buzzed on the desk. She didn't move to answer it. She already knew what it would say—reminders from Maxwell, logistics, contracts. A future that suddenly felt like paperwork instead of possibility.

She looked back at the inn's fireplace, still glowing from the logs Mabel had set earlier. Her aunt's photo sat above the mantle, smiling as if she already knew what Olivia hadn't figured out yet.

"I tried," Olivia said quietly. "I really did."

Her voice trembled. "But I don't know how to do both things. The woman who fights her way up… and the one who stays when her heart says to."

The fire popped softly, and for a moment, she imagined her aunt answering in the same calm voice that used to tell her that love wasn't weakness. That maybe success was about what you gave, not what you gained.

Olivia pressed a hand over her chest. "I miss you," she whispered. "And I think I'm losing everything you left me."

***

Across town, Ethan sat in his truck at the edge of the square, watching the lights flicker to life one by one. The festival tents were ready, the town alive with the kind of joy that should have filled him.

Instead, all he felt was the ache behind his ribs.

Rusty sat in the passenger seat, tail thumping softly, eyes half-closed. Ethan reached over to scratch behind his ears. "Looks like it's just you and me tonight, buddy."

The dog whined quietly, as if disagreeing.

Ethan smiled weakly. "Yeah, I know. I'm an idiot."

He leaned his head back against the seat, watching the snow swirl through the windshield. "I should've told her I loved her," he murmured.

"Before pride got in the way. Before I let her think she wasn't already part of this place."

But then he pictured her walking through the airport tomorrow, suitcase in hand, and headed toward skyscrapers and glass offices. He thought of the life she'd built long before Maplewood.

And he told himself what he always did when things broke: *You can't fix what doesn't want to stay.*

He turned the key, the engine rumbling to life. But even as he drove home, the lights in the rearview mirror looked like something he'd never stop looking back at.

***

At the same time, Olivia blew out the last candle in the inn's sitting room and stood at the window one final time. Snow fell thick and slow, blanketing the world in white.

Across the distance, she could see faint headlights disappearing down the road; they were the lights of a truck she recognized by heart.

For a second, she almost ran after it.

Instead, she whispered to the empty room, "Merry Christmas, Ethan."

And in another part of Maplewood, a man whispered to the falling snow, "Merry Christmas, Olivia."

Neither heard the other.

But both were looking at the same sky.

Chapter 15:

The Festival and Realization

Morning came soft and gold over Maplewood, the kind of Christmas Eve that looked painted—rooftops capped with snow, smoke curling from chimneys, the air sharp and clean.

Olivia stood at the window, still in her robe, watching the world below stir awake. The town square was already bustling. She could hear faint music overlayed with the sound of sleigh bells, laughter, and the steady hum of voices.

The courier never came.

Her papers still sat on the desk, unsigned. She'd spent the night staring at them, her pen uncapped, waiting for courage that never arrived.

Now, sunlight poured through the curtains, catching the edge of the page and turning it gold.

She closed the folder, set it aside, and whispered to herself, "One last look before I go."

***

When she stepped outside, the cold bit at her cheeks, but the air smelled like cinnamon and hope.

The square was alive. Booths lined the street, filled with handmade ornaments, knitted scarves, and cookies dusted with sugar. Mabel was manning the cider stand, cheeks rosy and eyes bright. Sophie ran through the crowd with a basket of candy canes, laughing as she handed them to children.

And everywhere, people called her name.

"Olivia! Merry Christmas!"

"Parker! You coming to the tree lighting later?"

"Couldn't have done this without you, dear!"

Each voice hit her heart like a bell.

She smiled, dazed, moving through the crowd. Every corner of Maplewood glowed; ribbons were tied to lampposts, snowflakes were strung across windows, and mistletoe was hanging just high enough to make people blush.

This was the world she'd helped bring to life.

The world she'd been ready to leave.

She paused by the stage, watching the choir sing. Children in oversized scarves swayed out of rhythm, one little boy belting every note like his life depended on it. The crowd clapped along, and something inside her chest loosened, just a little.

She turned slowly, her gaze drifting to the inn at the end of the street. Its windows were glowing and its door was open wide, with laughter spilling out from inside. Guests were coming and going, arms full of presents, faces full of joy.

Her aunt's inn.

Her aunt's dream.

It looked *alive* again.

And she'd almost sold it.

***

Mabel spotted her from across the square and waved. "There you are! I was starting to think you'd gone back to that big city of yours."

Olivia laughed, breath fogging in the cold. "Not yet."

"Well, thank heavens. We need you for the raffle drawing. And the hot chocolate booth. And possibly crowd control."

"Crowd control?"

"Only if the marshmallows run out," Mabel said with mock seriousness. "The townsfolk take that personally."

They both laughed, and for a fleeting second, everything felt right again.

As they walked toward the inn together, Mabel's arm looped through hers. The older woman leaned closer. "You look different today, Olivia."

"How so?"

"Like someone who finally stopped running."

Olivia opened her mouth to protest, but the words wouldn't come.

Because for the first time, she realized Mabel was right.

***

They reached the inn just as the bell above the door chimed, and warmth wrapped around them. The smell of pine and sugar cookies filled the air; garlands framed the hallways. A family laughed near the piano, their children banging at the keys with cheerful chaos.

Olivia stood still, taking it all in.

This wasn't just her aunt's legacy anymore. It was her own.

She could feel it in the laughter, in the light, in the way the walls seemed to breathe again.

And somewhere in that quiet knowing, she heard her aunt's voice, soft and certain: *You don't have to choose between doing well and doing good.*

Olivia blinked away the tears threatening to fall.

Maybe she didn't have to choose at all.

***

The Christmas Festival hit its peak by late afternoon.

Olivia carried a tray of cider Mabel had thrust into her hands, weaving through the crowd. She'd told herself she was doing one last favor, one last hour—but somehow that hour had stretched into three.

She passed Sophie, who was corralling a group of kids into the gingerbread contest, laughing as frosting exploded in every direction. A few feet away, the mayor was loudly losing an argument over cookie judges with Mrs. Halpern.

And at the center of it all, as always, was Ethan.

He stood by the main stage, sleeves rolled up, setting up a sound system with two volunteers. His breath misted in the cold air, cheeks flushed pink, hair dusted with snow.

Even from a distance, Olivia could see how he moved in that calm, steady, and capable way. She noticed the way people naturally turned to him for direction.

He hadn't seen her yet.

She could've walked away. Should have, maybe. But something in her refused to move.

When he finally turned, catching sight of her across the square, the world seemed to hold its breath.

For a moment, neither of them moved.

Then Ethan nodded and went back to work.

It shouldn't have hurt. But it did.

***

Mabel appeared at her elbow, following her gaze. "He's been here since dawn," she said quietly. "Wouldn't let anyone else lift a thing."

130

"I know," Olivia said softly.

"He says he doesn't do Christmas for himself. Says he does it for the town. But I think he's been doing it for someone in particular this year."

Olivia turned to her. "Mabel—"

The older woman just smiled sadly. "We all see it, dear. Everyone but you two."

Olivia's throat tightened. "I made a mess of everything."

"Maybe. But messes can be cleaned up." Mabel nudged her gently. "Go on. Help him with the stage before he electrocutes himself trying to prove he doesn't miss you."

***

Ethan was adjusting a cable when Olivia approached, her voice tentative. "That's not grounded properly."

He froze at the sound of her.

"I checked the power line last week," she continued, gesturing to the outlet. "It's reversed polarity. You'll blow the speaker if you—"

He glanced back, eyes meeting hers. "Didn't know I had an expert on hand."

"You do now," she said, managing a small smile.

For a second, something softened in his face. Then he handed her the cable. "Guess I could use a second pair of hands."

They worked in a silence that was mechanical and careful. But every brush of their shoulders, every shared glance felt heavier than it should.

Finally, the speaker crackled to life. The opening chords of *Silent Night* drifted out, filling the air with something fragile and beautiful.

Ethan stepped back, folding his arms. "You still got it," he said quietly.

Olivia exhaled. "You too."

For a moment, the noise of the festival faded, replaced by that same quiet that always seemed to settle between them, the kind that said everything words couldn't.

She turned to him. "Why are you still doing this?"

He frowned. "Doing what?"

"All of it. The work. The lights. The festival. When you could've just walked away."

He hesitated. "Because this town deserves it. Because it's home."

Her voice wavered. "And because of me?"

He didn't answer right away. Then, softly, "I don't do things halfway, Parker. Not even when it hurts."

Her chest tightened. "You always make it sound so simple."

"It is."

"No," she said, shaking her head. "It's terrifying."

Ethan's expression softened, a shadow of the man who'd once kissed her under mistletoe. "Maybe that's how you know it's real."

***

They stood there as the choir began to sing, their voices rising above the snow and lights. Olivia's eyes glistened as she watched families join hands, children lift candles, and laughter mingled with the music.

It wasn't just a festival. It was life, and it was messy, loud, and full of love she hadn't believed she deserved.

And suddenly she saw it clearly: This was what she'd been searching for all along.

The sky deepened into evening as the choir finished their last song. All around the square, the crowd began to hum with anticipation. This was the moment everyone had been waiting for.

Mayor Halpern climbed onto the stage, cheeks red from the cold, microphone in hand. "All right, Maplewood," he boomed. "It's time to light the tree!"

Applause rippled through the square.

Ethan adjusted the last wire connection while Olivia handed out candles for the countdown. People's faces glowed in the flicker of tiny flames, their breath misting like silver ribbons in the cold air.

The mayor grinned. "Three… two… one!"

The tree burst into light.

Strings of gold and white shimmered up the branches, ornaments glittered, and at the top, the star Sophie and Ethan had placed earlier burned brighter than anything Olivia had ever seen.

The crowd erupted in cheers. Carols swelled. Bells chimed from the church tower.

And for a long, breathless moment, Olivia forgot the city, the papers, the deadlines.

She just *felt*.

The laughter. The warmth. The way the light reflected in the snow.

And beside her stood Ethan, who was tired and proud, his face turned toward the glow. He had given everything to this small patch of the world and somehow made it feel infinite.

She turned to look at him, really look at him, and it hit her like a quiet truth: This was home. Not a place on a map, not a title or a paycheck.

Home was *him*. Home was Maplewood. Home was everything that made her heart ache and soften all at once.

Tears pricked her eyes before she could stop them. She blinked quickly, but Ethan noticed.

"Hey," he said gently. "You okay?"

She nodded, smiling through it. "I think so. I just… forgot how beautiful this could be."

He studied her for a moment, something unreadable in his eyes. "You didn't forget. You just didn't know yet."

His words undid her completely.

She had spent years chasing meaning, purpose, success—thinking she'd find it in skyscrapers and boardrooms. But it was here, all along, hidden in laughter and snowfall and the quiet steadiness of a man who never stopped showing up.

The music shifted to *Have Yourself a Merry Little Christmas,* slow and soft, and couples began to sway near the stage. Candles flickered, snow fell in lazy spirals, and for the first time in years, Olivia didn't feel like she was performing.

She just existed—warm, messy, and real.

Mabel passed by, eyes twinkling. "Funny thing about Christmas," she said with a wink. "It tends to sneak up on the people who need it most."

Olivia laughed through her tears. "You're impossible."

"Maybe. But I'm right."

As Mabel drifted away, Ethan turned to her again, his expression gentle. "You should be proud. You made this happen."

She shook her head. "We did."

They stood in silence then, side by side, watching as the town glowed brighter and brighter.

Somewhere deep inside, Olivia knew what she needed to do—not tomorrow, not later. *Now.*

Not for him. Not for her aunt. But for herself.

Because for the first time, she wasn't afraid of choosing happiness.

Chapter 16:

Grand Gesture

Olivia sat at her aunt's old desk, a mug of coffee going cold beside her, the sale papers open in front of her once more.

The courier had come yesterday, and she'd ignored the knock.

Now the envelope sat by the door, sealed but unsigned.

Her pen lay across the page like a question mark.

She'd spent most of the night staring at it, trying to convince herself to finish what she'd started. *One signature,* she told herself. *One clean break.*

But every time she tried to pick up the pen, her hand froze.

Because when she closed her eyes, she didn't see skyscrapers or conference rooms. She saw Maplewood: children laughing in the snow, Sophie's grin, Mabel's quiet faith, Ethan's eyes when he talked about home.

Her aunt's voice echoed faintly in her head: *You don't have to choose between doing well and doing good. Just remember which one fills you up more.*

Olivia reached for the pen again. This time, instead of signing, she drew a slow line through the words *Transfer of Ownership.*

Then she set the papers aside, exhaled shakily, and smiled for the first time in days.

She wasn't running anymore.

***

The sound of bells outside drew her to the window. The town was already awake, decorating the last booths, music rising like sunlight through the snow.

Christmas Eve.

The festival was hours away, and for once, she wasn't a guest or an outsider. She was part of it.

She pulled on her red coat, the one Ethan had said made her look like a candy cane, and stepped outside.

The cold bit at her cheeks, but it didn't sting. It felt *real*.

Mabel was on the porch, adjusting the garland with a knowing smile. "I had a feeling you weren't going anywhere."

"Guess I'm not," Olivia said.

Mabel patted her arm. "Good. Because we've got a full house, and someone needs to make the announcement at the lighting tonight."

Olivia blinked. "Announcement?"

"The town wants a few words from you—about your aunt, the inn, the festival. A proper dedication."

"Mabel, I—"

"Oh, don't start," she interrupted, eyes twinkling. "You've spent weeks fixing this place, helping us, keeping the spirit alive. It's your turn to speak."

Olivia hesitated. "I don't know what to say."

"Then say the truth."

Mabel winked and headed back inside, leaving Olivia standing in the crisp morning air, heart racing.

The truth.

That was the hardest part.

***

Hours later, the square was packed. The final carols had finished, candles glowed in mittened hands, and the stage lights flickered gold against the falling snow.

Olivia stood behind the curtain, her breath fogging the cold air. The mayor was finishing his introduction, his booming voice carrying through the square.

"—and none of this," he said, "would've been possible without a certain someone. A woman who brought life back to the Parker Inn, and maybe, if we're lucky, a little more Christmas magic to Maplewood. Please welcome Olivia Parker!"

Applause erupted, warm and thunderous.

Olivia stepped forward into the light.

And somewhere near the back, just beyond the glow of the stage, she saw him.

Ethan, standing still among the crowd, watching her like she was something fragile he didn't dare reach for again.

Her heart skipped.

It was time.

***

For a heartbeat, the only sound was the wind through the garlands and the soft creak of the microphone stand as she adjusted it.

The square was full of faces lit by candles, scarves pulled high, snowflakes settling in hair and eyelashes. Every pair of eyes was on her.

Olivia took a breath. "Hi," she said, her voice catching slightly. "I'm... Olivia Parker. Some of you know me as the woman who accidentally turned a plumbing disaster into a gingerbread contest."

Laughter rippled through the crowd, easing the knot in her chest.

She smiled. "When I first came here, I told myself it would be a quick trip. A little paperwork, a little nostalgia, and then I'd head back to New York—back to the life I'd built. I had plans, a schedule, a perfectly organized list of goals."

She glanced toward the inn, its windows glowing warmly behind the trees. "But then Maplewood happened."

A soft murmur ran through the crowd.

"I don't think I realized what this place meant until it was almost too late," she continued. "I came here expecting to manage an ending—to sell something that belonged to someone I loved. But what I found was… a beginning."

Her voice wavered, and she swallowed hard. "My aunt built the Parker Inn as a haven for anyone who needed to feel at home, even for one night. She believed home wasn't a building or a business. It was the people who fill it."

She looked out at the crowd. Mabel near the front, Sophie waving from the steps, the mayor wiping at his eyes. And then, her gaze found Ethan.

He stood near the back, arms folded, snow glinting in his hair, his expression unreadable but his eyes burning bright.

Her breath trembled. "I almost forgot that," she said softly, eyes never leaving him. "I almost sold it because I thought success only counted if it came with titles and paychecks. But the truth is, every smile I've seen here, every laugh echoing through the inn, every person who stopped by just to help, that's worth more than any promotion."

The crowd was silent now, every ear tuned to her words.

She stepped closer to the microphone. "So, I'm not selling the Parker Inn."

There was a collective gasp, followed by bright cheers that filled the square like fireworks.

Olivia laughed, a sound halfway between relief and disbelief, tears stinging her eyes. "I'm staying because it's *right,* because this is where I belong."

She pressed a hand to her heart. "My aunt's legacy deserves more than a transaction. It deserves a heartbeat. And somehow, you all gave that back to me. So thank you for reminding me what home feels like. For making me remember who I am."

The mayor started clapping first, then Mabel, then the entire crowd joined in, their applause rolling like thunder through the square.

But Olivia only saw Ethan.

He hadn't moved, hadn't clapped. He just stood there, watching her like he was afraid that if he blinked, she'd disappear again.

Their eyes met, and something inside her steadied.

She smiled—small, sincere, trembling. The kind of smile that said *I'm here.*

Ethan's expression flickered between surprise and disbelief, and then something softer: hope.

For a second, it was just them.

The past between them still hung heavy, but for the first time, it felt like something they could carry together.

***

When the crowd began to disperse, people came to hug her, thank her, and cheer her name. Mabel pressed a handkerchief into her palm. Sophie threw her arms around her waist.

"You're really staying?" the girl asked, eyes wide.

"I am," Olivia said, voice steady. "For good."

And somewhere near the edge of the square, Ethan turned away because he didn't trust himself not to walk straight to her.

***

The crowd slowly thinned, drifting toward the food stalls and carolers, their laughter echoing through the square. The Parker Inn's windows glowed brighter than ever, candles flickering in every room, wreaths shining in the soft light.

Olivia stood on the stage a little longer, watching people hug and smile, letting the applause fade into memory. It felt like waking up after a long dream; everything was sharper, clearer, more *real*.

She took a deep breath of cold air. The snow was falling again, fine and steady, landing softly in her hair. For the first time in months, her chest didn't ache.

She had made her choice.

And yet, as she stepped down from the stage, she found herself searching the crowd.

Mabel was near the cider booth, smiling proudly. Sophie was busy dragging a friend toward the carousel. But Ethan—

He was gone.

Her heart stuttered.

She turned slowly, scanning the edges of the square until she caught sight of him by the tree line, standing near the old lamppost. His posture was careful, guarded, like he wasn't sure if he was allowed to stay.

Before she could lose her nerve, she crossed the snow.

***

Ethan heard her boots crunching behind him, but didn't turn. His hands were shoved deep into his coat pockets, his breath fogging in the cold.

"I didn't think you'd come find me," he said quietly.

"I wasn't sure if you wanted me to."

"I wasn't sure either," he admitted.

For a moment, neither spoke. The wind moved through the trees, carrying faint strains of music from the square.

Finally, she said, "You heard what I said up there."

"I did."

"I meant every word."

He nodded slowly. "You're really staying?"

"Yes," she said, voice steady. "I tore up the papers this morning. The inn's not for sale. It never was, not really. I just... didn't know how to belong anywhere that wasn't built out of ambition."

He looked at her then, finally meeting her eyes. "And now?"

"Now," she said softly, "I'm done measuring success by what I can lose."

Ethan exhaled, a shaky laugh escaping him. "You sure know how to make a man question every good decision he's ever made."

She smiled. "Maybe you should make one more bad one, then."

He frowned slightly. "Like what?"

"Like forgiving me."

The words hung there, fragile and brave.

Ethan studied her for a long moment, the snow catching in his hair, melting on his collar. Then, quietly, "I already did."

Her breath hitched. "You did?"

"Yeah," he said, his voice rough. "Somewhere between the gingerbread disaster and you showing up in that ridiculous red coat."

She laughed through her tears, pressing a hand to her mouth. "You really are impossible."

"Maybe," he said. "But I'm yours, if you'll have me."

That undid her completely.

She stepped closer, the air between them humming with everything they hadn't said for weeks. "I was hoping you'd say that."

Ethan reached up, brushing a snowflake from her cheek with his thumb. "You're freezing."

"Then you'd better do something about it," she whispered.

And this time, when he kissed her, it wasn't a question or a maybe. It was a promise.

The world around them blurred.

When they finally pulled apart, both were smiling.

Ethan rested his forehead against hers. "So... what now?"

Olivia glanced toward the glowing inn, laughter spilling through its open doors. "Now," she said softly, "we go home."

Chapter 17:

Emotional Reunion

Olivia stood by the window of her aunt's office, still wearing her coat. The fire in the grate had burned down to embers, but she couldn't bring herself to sleep. Her body was tired, but her heart... her heart was restless.

She'd made her speech. She'd made her choice.

But there was still one thing left unfinished.

Ethan.

He'd kissed her under the lamppost, and for the first time, she'd felt completely steady. But the moment had been swept away by the crowd, by the noise, by everything that wasn't them. He'd walked her back to the inn, gentle and quiet, and then just as she'd found the courage to say everything she'd been holding back, he'd touched her cheek, smiled, and then he'd left.

Now, standing there with snow dusting the windowsill, she realized that if she didn't tell him tonight, she never would.

She grabbed her scarf, her gloves, and stepped outside.

The air was freezing. The streets were almost empty now. The tree still shimmered in the distance, its star glowing faintly against the dark.

Ethan's truck wasn't by the workshop. Not at the square. Not by the barn.

Then she saw a faint light glowing from the greenhouse behind his farmhouse, half-hidden by snow.

Of course.

She crossed the yard slowly, boots crunching, breath fogging in front of her. Inside the glasshouse, she could see him.

He looked calm, but tired. A man trying to fill the silence with work.

She hesitated at the door. Then, before she could talk herself out of it, she pushed it open.

The warm, earthy air hit her, heavy with pine and soil. Ethan turned, startled.

"Olivia?"

"Hi," she said softly. "I figured I'd find you here."

He wiped his hands on a rag, setting down a watering can. "You should be inside. It's freezing."

"I couldn't sleep."

He gave a short, cautious smile. "Festival hangover?"

"Something like that," she said, taking a step closer.

The silence between them wasn't angry anymore. Just careful. This was the quiet before truth.

"I wanted to thank you," she began.

"For what?"

"For staying. For helping with the festival. For... not walking away, even when I gave you every reason to."

Ethan's gaze softened, though he said nothing.

Olivia swallowed hard. "I've been running my whole life," she admitted. "Every time something got too real, I'd find a new goal, a new reason to move. I told myself it was ambition. But really... it was fear."

Ethan's brow furrowed. "Fear of what?"

Her voice shook. "Of standing still. Of choosing something—or someone—that mattered more than success. Because what if I failed at that, too?"

He was quiet for a long moment, his eyes searching hers. "You think loving someone is failure?"

"I think it's the only thing I didn't know how to be good at," she whispered.

Ethan took a step forward, closing the distance between them. "You don't have to be good at it, Olivia. You just have to *want* it."

***

For a long moment, Ethan didn't move. Then, he took another step closer, his voice low. "You don't have to say this just because of the festival, or the speech, or Christmas. I don't need a grand gesture."

"I know," Olivia said. "That's why I'm here."

He studied her face, noticing the glint of sincerity in her eyes and the tremble in her voice.

She continued softly, "When I first got here, I thought you were impossible."

He chuckled, the sound quiet and rough. "Most people do."

"You were stubborn and infuriating and so sure I didn't belong here."

"You told me you didn't," he reminded her.

"I know. But you were right," she said, shaking her head, a small, disbelieving laugh escaping her.

Her voice dropped. "I met you. And suddenly, everything I thought I wanted didn't matter the same way anymore."

Ethan's jaw tightened. He looked away for a moment, toward the tiny pine trees lined neatly behind him. "You made it hard not to fall for you, Parker," he admitted finally.

Her breath caught. "What did you just say?"

He turned back to her, eyes dark and unguarded. "I tried not to. I told myself you were temporary—a New York hurricane just passing through. I thought if I kept my head down, you'd leave before I got stupid enough to care."

Her pulse stumbled. "And?"

He exhaled, a shaky laugh. "Turns out I got stupid anyway."

Olivia smiled through a sudden rush of tears. "You fell for me."

"I did," he said simply. "Despite every warning sign. Despite knowing you'd probably go back to your life, and I'd be here picking up pieces of what might've been."

She stepped closer, voice barely a whisper. "Why didn't you tell me?"

"Because I thought you needed freedom more than you needed me."

That broke something open in her.

She closed the distance between them until she was standing inches away. "I thought I needed freedom too," she whispered. "But I think what I really needed was *peace.* And somehow, you're the only person who makes me feel like I can stop running."

Ethan's throat bobbed as he swallowed. "You mean that?"

She nodded, tears spilling now. "I mean every word. You're what feels like home, Ethan. Not the inn, not the town—*you.*"

He reached up, brushing away a tear with his thumb, his hand lingering against her cheek. "You sure you want to be tied down to a man who spends his Christmas Eve fixing lights and overfeeding reindeer?"

"I'm sure," she said, smiling through her tears. "Because the only thing I want to fix now is us."

For the first time in weeks, his smile reached his eyes. "You always did like a challenge."

"Then let's start there."

Ethan cupped her face, his palms warm against her chilled skin. "You have no idea how long I've wanted to hear you say that."

"Then don't waste another second," she whispered.

He didn't.

The kiss started slowly and then deepened, gathering all the things they hadn't said, hadn't dared to feel. The world outside the greenhouse faded: the snow, the wind, the hum of distant music. All that remained was the quiet rhythm of their breathing and the steady beat of two hearts finally finding each other.

When they parted, their foreheads rested together, breaths mingling in the cold air. Olivia's hands slid into his coat, gripping his shirt like she needed to make sure he was real.

Ethan laughed softly, his voice rough. "You're shaking."

"I've been holding my breath for weeks," she murmured. "Guess I can finally stop."

He smiled, pressing a kiss to her forehead. "You're sure about staying? No regrets, no second thoughts?"

She looked up at him, eyes bright. "If I ever start to forget, just remind me what this feels like."

He brushed his thumb over her lower lip, grinning. "That I can do."

Outside, the storm had eased, leaving the world still and bright. Through the fogged glass, the first blush of dawn touched the snow, painting everything in shades of rose and gold.

Olivia leaned into him, resting her head against his chest. "It's Christmas morning," she whispered.

"Best one I've ever had," he said.

They stood there for a long while, the greenhouse bathed in soft light, the scent of pine and earth around them. The kind of silence that felt like a prayer.

Finally, Olivia pulled back just enough to look at him. "So," she said, teasing, "does this mean you'll finally let me help fix the porch railing?"

Ethan raised a brow. "Not a chance."

She laughed, swatting his arm. "You're impossible."

"Yeah," he said, smiling as he drew her close again. "But you're stuck with me now."

She didn't argue.

Chapter 18:

Epilogue Setup

Winter lingered in Maplewood, but it wasn't the gray, lonely kind anymore.

This was the kind of winter that sparkled with soft snow on rooftops, lights still twined around lampposts, and laughter spilling from shop doors.

And at the heart of it all, the Parker Inn had come alive again.

Its sign gleamed fresh and new, hand-painted by one of the local artists: *The Parker Inn – Est. 1972. Reimagined 2025.*

Olivia stood in the middle of the lobby, hands on her hips, a streak of paint on her cheek, and a look of satisfied exhaustion on her face.

"You realize," came a familiar voice from behind her, "you've been standing in that exact spot for ten minutes."

She turned, smiling. Ethan leaned in the doorway, arms crossed, a hammer tucked into his tool belt.

"I'm just admiring the work," she said.

"Our work," he corrected, stepping closer.

She tilted her head. "You mean *my* design plans and *your* stubborn refusal to use power tools?"

He smirked. "You can't improve on perfection."

"Uh-huh." She laughed, shaking her head. "If perfection means spending four hours arguing about curtain rods, then sure."

"Hey," he said, picking up a stray piece of garland from the floor. "You're the one who wanted them to 'match the emotional tone of the entryway.'"

"It's called ambiance," she said, mock serious. "You should try it sometime."

Ethan grinned. "You're something else, Parker."

"Don't I know it."

They stood there for a beat, surrounded by the glow of their handiwork. Every brushstroke, every nail, every lightbulb was a quiet testament to what they'd built together.

"You ready for the grand reopening?" Ethan asked.

Olivia nodded, her smile softening. "Almost. Just waiting on one last thing."

"What's that?"

She turned toward the window, watching as the first guests of the season—an older couple holding hands—walked up the path, their breath white in the cold air. "People," she said. "Laughter. Stories. The kind of life my aunt always wanted this place to have."

Ethan followed her gaze, then looked back at her. "You've done her proud, you know."

Olivia swallowed the lump rising in her throat. "I hope so."

He touched her hand gently. "I know so."

***

Renovating an inn, Olivia quickly learned, was more about patience, and the patience, it turned out, came mostly from Ethan.

He'd show up at dawn with cocoa in hand, smelling like pine and cold air, his truck full of lumber and good intentions. She'd already be inside, hair tied up, floor plans spread across the counter like battle maps.

"Don't even think about changing that wall," he'd say.

"I'm not changing it," she'd answer. "Just… expanding it."

"That's still changing it, Parker."

"Semantics."

It became their rhythm. Her vision, his craftsmanship; her sketches, his steady hands. Between the two of them, the Parker Inn began to glow again.

It stopped feeling like work somewhere along the way. It became *homecoming*.

***

One afternoon, as snow sifted through the windows, Olivia climbed a ladder to hang a set of fairy lights above the front desk.

"Little higher," Ethan said from below, holding the ladder steady.

"If I go any higher, I'll be part of the ceiling," she called down.

"You said you wanted sparkle."

"I wanted ambiance," she corrected. "There's a difference."

Ethan grinned up at her. "Same thing in my book."

"Your book doesn't have enough adjectives."

"Your book doesn't have enough common sense."

She laughed so hard the ladder shook slightly. Ethan grabbed the side rails immediately. "Hey—careful!"

"I'm fine!"

"Parker, I swear—"

Too late. A bulb slipped from her hand, bounced once, and shattered on the floor.

They stared at it for a moment before both burst out laughing.

Ethan sighed. "You're lucky I like chaos."

"No," she said, climbing down and brushing snowflakes from her hair. "I'm lucky you like *me*."

He smiled, shaking his head. "That too."

***

By evening, the inn was glowing again. Candles were lit, the walls were fresh, and lights were twinkling softly. They stood together in the center of the lobby, tools forgotten, watching the way the firelight caught the new varnish on the wood.

Olivia leaned against his shoulder. "It's perfect," she whispered.

Ethan tilted his head. "Still think you'll miss the city?"

She considered it for a moment, then smiled. "I think I'll miss the noise sometimes. But Maplewood has its own kind of noise."

"Hey, that wiring saved your lobby."

She nudged him. "I know. And you saved a lot more than that."

He turned toward her, expression soft. "You did the saving, Parker. I just held the ladder."

***

The next morning, a light snow began to fall again. The inn's *Grand Reopening* sign gleamed by the door.

Guests arrived with suitcases and smiles; Mabel handled the front desk like she'd been born behind it. Children ran through the halls laughing, and Sophie strung paper snowflakes along the banister.

Olivia stood by the fireplace, watching it all unfold.

It wasn't the future she'd planned; it was better.

And as Ethan crossed the room to hand her a cup of cocoa, the faintest trace of sawdust still clinging to his jacket, she thought: *This is exactly what love builds.*

***

The evening of the reopening felt like something out of a dream.

The inn was alive again: fireplaces flickering in every room, garlands framing the windows, soft music floating through the halls. Guests milled about the lobby with mugs of mulled cider, their laughter curling like smoke into the rafters. The chandelier glittered above them, catching every spark of light.

Olivia stood by the front desk in a cranberry-red dress, her hair swept up loosely, a sprig of evergreen pinned just above her ear. For once, she wasn't worrying about details or schedules—she was just *present*.

Mabel bustled past, balancing a tray of gingerbread cookies. "You did it, dear," she said, eyes shining. "She'd be proud."

Olivia smiled, the lump in her throat thick. "I hope she's watching."

"Oh, she is," Mabel said with certainty. "You can feel it in the walls." Then she winked. "And if she's not, I'll haunt you for her."

Olivia laughed, wiping at her eyes. "Deal."

Across the room, Ethan was talking with the mayor, sleeves rolled up, tie slightly crooked, a hammer still peeking from his pocket as if he might fix something mid-conversation. When he caught Olivia watching, he tipped his head toward the porch.

She slipped outside.

***

The night was clear. Music and laughter drifted faintly from the open door.

Ethan joined her, handing over a mug of cocoa. "You survived the crowd."

"Barely." She smiled. "They're good people."

"They're *your* people now."

She looked out over Maplewood. "It still feels strange hearing that."

"Give it time," he said. "It'll stop feeling strange and start feeling like breathing."

"I spent so many years chasing everything that was supposed to make me happy. But somehow it all led me here." Olivia said.

Ethan smiled faintly. "Funny how that works."

She turned toward him. "Do you ever wonder what would've happened if I'd never come back?"

He shook his head. "No point in wondering. You did. That's all that matters."

Olivia set her mug down on the railing, the steam curling into the night. "I want to build something real here. Keep my aunt's spirit alive, but make it our own."

"You already are," he said. "And you've got a whole town behind you. Including one very stubborn handyman who happens to be crazy about you."

She laughed softly. "Lucky me."

He leaned closer. "Lucky both of us."

***

The town clock struck nine, its bells echoing through the snow. Somewhere inside, someone started singing *O Holy Night*. Lights from the inn spilled across the porch, wrapping them in gold.

Ethan slipped an arm around her waist, drawing her close. "You realize," he murmured, "this place is never going to be quiet again."

"I'm counting on it."

He chuckled. "You're sure you're ready for forever?"

Olivia looked up at him, eyes bright. "I already said yes to Maplewood. Saying yes to you was the easy part."

He kissed her then, and it was slow and sure, the kind of kiss that didn't need an audience or a holiday to make it special. When they parted, snowflakes clung to their lashes like tiny stars.

Inside, laughter rang out again; outside, the world was hushed and perfect.

Olivia leaned her head on his shoulder, watching the light spill across the snow. "Merry Christmas, Ethan."

He kissed her hair. "Welcome home, Olivia."

Chapter 19:

Christmas Morning

The first light of Christmas morning crept through the curtains in threads of gold. Inside the Parker Inn, everything was still—the fire burned low, the clock ticked softly, and the scent of cinnamon lingered in the air.

Olivia woke slowly, the kind of waking that came not from alarm but from peace. For a moment, she didn't move.

It had been years since she'd woken up somewhere that *felt* like home.

She smiled to herself and sat up, pulling on a sweater and fuzzy socks. She could still feel the coolness of the floorboards through the socks as she padded to the window. Outside, the town still slept beneath a quilt of snow. The Christmas lights twinkled faintly against the gray morning, like stars that refused to fade.

Downstairs, she could hear faint movement. Someone was stirring the fire, and there was the creak of a door.

Ethan.

She grinned and followed the sound, wrapping her robe tighter around her.

When she reached the lobby, she stopped in the doorway.

Ethan stood by the hearth, coaxing the flames back to life, his hair tousled, his flannel shirt rumpled. A mug of cocoa steamed on the table beside him. The morning light caught him just right.

It hit her all at once: This was what love looked like when it wasn't performing.

"Good morning," she said softly.

He turned, startled, then smiled. "You're up early."

"So are you."

He shrugged. "Couldn't sleep. The fire was dying."

Olivia crossed the room and took the other mug waiting on the table—hers, already made just the way she liked it. "You're dangerously good at that," she said, taking a sip.

"At making cocoa?"

"At knowing things you shouldn't," she teased.

Ethan grinned. "Perks of small-town living. We notice things."

She leaned against the mantel beside him. "It's beautiful out there," she said softly. "Quiet."

He nodded, eyes on the window. "Maplewood's always quiet on Christmas morning. It's like the whole town takes a breath at once."

They stood there for a moment, side by side, the fire crackling gently between them.

Olivia glanced around the room. She looked at the garlands she'd hung, the stockings Sophie had embroidered, and the star atop the inn's small tree glittering in the corner. Every bit of it felt alive, loved, *theirs*.

"You did good, Parker," Ethan said quietly, as if reading her thoughts.

She smiled. "*We* did."

He turned to her then, his gaze soft and searching. "You really staying? No second thoughts, no Manhattan regrets?"

"None," she said simply. "This is where I want to be. Where I'm meant to be."

The words felt different this time—not a decision, but a truth.

Ethan exhaled, a small smile tugging at his lips. "I love you, Olivia."

"I love you, Ethan."

***

The inn had never felt so warm.

Olivia and Ethan lingered by the fire, cocoa mugs in hand, as soft music played from the old radio on the mantle—a crackling rendition of *Have Yourself a Merry Little Christmas.*

The kind of song that made the world feel small and safe.

Ethan poked at the fire one last time, then leaned back against the sofa. "Sophie's probably opening presents with her friends by now," he said, smiling faintly. "Mabel's probably making a second pie she swears isn't for breakfast."

Olivia laughed. "And you're here pretending you're not waiting for me to burn breakfast."

He raised an eyebrow. "Experience has taught me to let you near the kitchen only under supervision."

"Fair," she admitted.

They sat in comfortable silence for a while, watching the flames dance. Then Olivia turned toward the small tree in the corner, the one they'd decorated together last night after the guests had gone to bed. It leaned slightly to the left, but its lights twinkled merrily, and the handmade ornaments from Maplewood's children hung proudly between store-bought glass baubles.

She reached beneath it and pulled out a small box wrapped in brown paper and tied with twine.

Ethan blinked. "What's this?"

"Your Christmas gift."

He smiled warily. "You didn't have to—"

"I wanted to." She handed it to him, her heart thudding as he took it.

He untied the twine slowly, unfolding the paper with the same care he gave to everything. Inside was a simple glass ornament, round and clear, with a small pressed sprig of holly inside.

He looked up, puzzled but smiling. "It's beautiful."

"It belonged to my aunt," Olivia said softly. "It was her favorite ornament. She used to hang it in the window every Christmas morning so the light would hit it just right. She said it reminded her that joy's always made brighter by a little bit of light."

Ethan turned it in his hand, the morning sun glinting through the glass. "It's perfect."

"I want you to have it," she said. "Because without you… I don't think the light would've come back here at all."

For a moment, neither of them spoke. The air between them felt heavy with all the words they'd said and all the ones they hadn't needed to.

Then Ethan cleared his throat, a little gruffly. "You're making it hard to top that, Parker."

"Good," she teased gently. "I like winning."

He chuckled and reached into his jacket pocket. "Then maybe this is a tie."

He handed her a small box, the kind that wasn't bought but *made* of smoothed wood, hinges slightly imperfect, and the grain visible like lines of a story.

Olivia opened it carefully.

Inside was a star.

Hand-carved, simple, sanded smooth, and strung with a bit of twine.

She lifted it out, holding it up toward the firelight. The carved edges caught the glow, each ridge shining faintly gold.

"Ethan…" she whispered. "You made this?"

He nodded, rubbing the back of his neck. "It's the same kind of wood I used for the inn's new sign."

Her voice wavered. "It's beautiful."

"I wasn't going for beautiful," he said softly. "I was going for something that would last."

She looked up at him then, eyes shimmering. "You realize this means you've just one-upped me, right?"

He grinned. "I'll take the win."

Olivia laughed, tucking the ornament safely into her palm. "Thank you. Really."

He met her gaze, serious now. "It's not just a gift, Liv. The star—it's… us. Not perfect. But built to shine, even when things get dark."

Her throat tightened. "You and your metaphors."

"Hey," he said softly, brushing a loose strand of hair from her face, "I learned from the best."

She smiled, her eyes bright with tears. "You really did."

***

The inn was still quiet, and for once, there was no list waiting on Olivia's desk, no phone buzzing with reminders.

Only this. Only him. Only home.

She traced the edge of the wooden star in her hand, feeling the smooth grooves where Ethan's knife had shaped it. The thought of him working or it late at night, in that old workshop that always smelled of pine and sawdust, made her heart swell.

When she looked up, Ethan was already watching her.

"What?" she asked softly.

He shrugged, a slow smile forming. "Just making sure you're real."

"I could say the same thing," she whispered.

He chuckled, leaning back on the couch. "You know, I've spent a lot of Christmas mornings out in the cold. Delivering trees, fixing frozen pipes, and helping Mabel untangle lights. Never thought I'd end one here, sitting next to a woman who changed everything."

Olivia tilted her head, teasing. "Everything? That's a lot of credit."

"Not enough," he said.

The sincerity in his voice made her pulse skip.

Ethan set his mug down and turned toward her fully. "When you showed up, I didn't know what to do with you," he admitted. "You were... lightning in heels. All plans and lists and coffee that tasted like ambition."

She laughed, blushing. "I'll take that as a compliment?"

"It is," he said. "Because you walked into my life and flipped it on its head. You made this town wake up again. Made me wake up again."

Her smile faltered, softening. "Ethan..."

He shook his head. "I used to think people like you never stayed. That I shouldn't get close because it'd hurt too much when you left. But you proved me wrong. You stayed."

Olivia reached out, taking his hand. "Because you made me want to."

He smiled, eyes bright and unguarded. "You're my Christmas miracle, Olivia."

The words fell quiet and sure, the kind that didn't need to be shouted to be true.

Her breath hitched. "Say that again."

He leaned in, his forehead brushing hers. "You're my Christmas miracle."

This time, she kissed him before he could say anything more. The fire flared as if in applause, shadows dancing on the walls.

When they finally pulled apart, Olivia laughed softly, her voice a whisper. "If this is what miracles look like, I'm never leaving Maplewood."

Ethan smiled, tracing her jaw with his thumb. "Good. Because I'm not letting you."

Outside, the town bells began to ring, echoing through the crisp morning air. She could hear distant laughter mingling with the footfalls of children running down snowy streets. The smell of cinnamon and pine was rising with the sun.

But here, in this quiet room filled with warmth and light, time felt like it had stopped.

Her aunt's words whispered back through memory: *Home isn't a place. It's the people who make you believe you belong.*

And for the first time in her life, Olivia truly did.

Chapter 20:

Epilogue (One Year Later)

Snow had returned to Maplewood, soft and steady, blanketing the town in white. But this year, it didn't feel quiet.

The *Maplewood Christmas Festival* had doubled in size with new stalls, brighter lights, and enough tinsel to make even Mabel declare victory over last year's stockpile. And at the heart of it all stood the Parker Inn, once fading, now radiant.

Its windows glowed warm against the winter dusk, wreaths shining on every door, garlands wrapping the banisters like ribbons of evergreen. A new wooden sign hung proudly from the post:

"The Parker Inn – Where Every Guest Finds Home."

Inside, the lobby buzzed with joy. Guests bustled in and out, stamping snow from their boots, greeted by a cheerful Sophie, now the inn's official "junior hostess," as she'd proudly titled herself.

Mabel manned the front desk with her usual blend of charm and authority, fussing over the check-in list while pretending not to.

And behind it all, Olivia Parker moved like sunlight.

She carried herself differently now with the ease of someone *rooted*. Her red scarf trailed over her shoulder as she arranged cookies on the welcome tray. The engagement ring on her hand caught the light, delicate and simple, carved in gold by one of the town's artisans.

She smiled as she adjusted a vase of pine boughs. "Mabel, remind me— did we set enough tables for the choir dinner tonight?"

Mabel huffed. "Of course. And before you ask, yes, the cider's warming, and no, I didn't let the mayor sneak any early."

Olivia laughed. "You're a saint."

"I'm underpaid," Mabel countered.

The bell above the door jingled, and Olivia turned.

Ethan stepped in, snow dusting his shoulders, his scarf slightly askew. He carried two boxes—one marked *Supplies,* the other labeled *Absolutely Not Pie.*

Olivia arched an eyebrow. "That second one looks suspiciously pie-shaped."

He grinned. "Mabel told me to bring it. Said it's 'definitely not breakfast dessert.'"

Mabel sniffed. "It's for the raffle."

"Uh-huh." Olivia smiled. "Sure it is."

Ethan crossed to her, setting the boxes down on the counter. "You've been running around since dawn," he said softly. "When's the part where you actually enjoy your own festival?"

"After I'm sure everything's perfect."

He brushed a strand of hair from her cheek. "Newsflash, Parker—it already is."

Olivia leaned in, eyes bright. "You're biased."

"Completely," he said.

***

By evening, the town square glowed brighter than any star in the sky.

Children darted between booths holding candied apples, the choir sang carols in front of the gazebo, and snowflakes swirled like confetti through strings of golden lights.

Olivia stood near the cider stand, wrapped in a thick coat and scarf, watching the scene unfold. Her cheeks were pink from the cold and her eyes were bright from something deeper—contentment.

Everywhere she looked, she saw echoes of love and effort: the garlands Ethan had strung across the square; the handmade ornaments Gideon and his friends had painted; the bakery's stall filled with gingerbread houses modeled after Maplewood landmarks.

And at the center, just like last year, stood the towering Christmas tree. This one was twice as tall as last year's and covered in shimmering ribbons and silver bells.

Ethan's handiwork.

He was near the stage now, giving instructions to two volunteers about the lights. His sleeves were rolled up despite the cold, his laugh carrying easily through the chatter.

She watched him for a long moment, smiling to herself.

A year ago, she'd been the city girl who planned to sell everything and leave before the snow melted. Now she knew the name of every vendor, every child, every neighbor. And she had Ethan, the man who'd built her a life out of lumber, laughter, and love.

Mabel appeared beside her, handing her a mug of steaming cider. "Don't just stand there like a proud mama hen," she teased. "Go make sure your fiancé isn't electrocuting himself again."

Olivia laughed. "That was one time."

"Mm-hmm. And it almost took out the gazebo lights."

Shaking her head, Olivia made her way toward the stage, weaving through the crowd. The music shifted to a slower carol, and people began gathering near the big tree, ready for the lighting ceremony.

Ethan spotted her as she approached, his smile breaking wide and easy. "You made it before I set the whole thing on fire," he said.

"I'd call that progress."

He reached for her gloved hand, squeezing it gently. "You ready?"

"For the lighting or for the chaos that follows?"

"Both."

"Then yes."

He grinned. "That's my girl."

***

The mayor took the stage, his voice booming through the square. "All right, Maplewood! This year's festival wouldn't exist without the people who make this town shine brighter than any tree—and none more so than our very own Olivia Parker and Ethan Cole!"

"Last year," the mayor continued, "we lit this tree in honor of the Parker legacy. This year, we light it in celebration of what happens when hope takes root. When love stays."

Ethan reached for the switch, then looked at Olivia. "You want to do the honors?"

She hesitated, smiling. "Together?"

He nodded.

Their fingers intertwined over the handle.

"Three... two... one!"

The lights flared to life, cascading up the tree in ripples of gold and white. The crowd gasped, then broke into applause and laughter. Bells chimed, music swelled, and snow began to fall, as if the sky itself wanted to join in.

Olivia tilted her head back, snowflakes catching in her hair. "It's even more beautiful than last year," she whispered.

Ethan glanced down at her, his voice soft. "So are you."

She looked at him, heart full. "You realize this is starting to sound like a Hallmark movie."

He grinned. "Good. Those always end well."

***

Olivia and Ethan walked the quiet streets hand in hand, their boots crunching through the thin crust of ice. The air smelled of pine and smoke. Behind them, the inn's windows glowed, golden against the dark.

"You did it again," Ethan said softly.

"We did it," she corrected. "You built the stage, remember?"

He chuckled. "And you made me use fairy lights instead of floodlamps. I think you win that one."

They paused at the edge of the square where the snow lay untouched. A single lamp burned above them, throwing a ring of light around their footprints.

Olivia tilted her head back, watching flakes melt against the lamplight. "Do you ever think about what life would've been like if I'd sold the inn?"

Ethan's voice was quiet. "Sometimes. Usually when I'm trying to remember what it felt like to be stupid."

She smiled, nudging him. "You weren't stupid. You just didn't know how stubborn I could be."

"Oh, I knew," he said, laughter rumbling low in his chest. "It was half the reason I fell for you."

Her breath caught in the cold air. "Half?"

"The other half," he murmured, brushing a snowflake from her hair, "was how you made this place shine again."

They stood there for a long time, the world slowing around them, snow soft against their coats. Olivia reached into her pocket and pulled out something small—his carved wooden star, now polished smooth with time.

"I kept it by the window," she said. "Every morning, it catches the first bit of light."

He smiled. "Still holding up?"

"Better than ever." She pressed it into his palm. "I thought maybe we could hang it together this year. You know—tradition."

Ethan turned the star over in his hand, his thumb tracing the worn twine. "You realize that means I have to carve a new one every year now."

"That's the idea."

He looked up at her, eyes bright with something tender and steady. "You really want to keep doing this? Festivals, guests, sawdust in my hair?"

"All of it," she said. "Forever sounds about right. I mean, we're engaged, aren't we?"

The corners of his mouth lifted. "Good. Because I already told the mayor next year's tree's going to need a stronger foundation."

She laughed, the sound soft and clear in the still night. "You're incorrigible."

"And you," he said, pulling her close, "are my Christmas miracle. Still."

The words came out like a vow—quiet, certain, true.

Olivia's eyes filled with light. "You're mine too."

He kissed her then, beneath the lamp and the falling snow, slow and sure. Around them, the town slept, wrapped in warmth and memory.

When they finally parted, she rested her forehead against his. "So… what happens now?"

Ethan smiled, his breath misting between them. "Now? We go home."

Together they turned toward the inn, their footsteps side by side, fading into the snow. The windows glowed brighter as they approached, and through the glass, the ornaments sparkled—the glass holly sphere and the wooden star shining next to each other, light pouring through both.

Above them, the bells from the church tower began to ring at midnight. Christmas again.

And in Maplewood, it always would be.

Printed in Dunstable, United Kingdom

73363662R00100